"I don't like being set up."

Matthew spoke in an oddly ominous smooth tone. In one swift angry movement he had gripped her shoulders. There was a hard glinting brightness in his eyes as he stared down at her. "Was it your own idea? Or is the camera artist your boyfriend?"

Deborah had reached an indifferent calm after the catastrophe of the night and was taken completely off guard. "Look—" she finally began, struggling to free herself in vain.

"No," he said fiercely. "You look. I recognize your pitch now. Blackmail, isn't it? I'll have to pay up—but first I want a little more value for my money."

There was no mistaking his intent, even if his eyes hadn't underlined it with a swift stripping glance over her....

CHARLOTTE LAMB

illusion

Harlequin Books

TORONTO • LONDON • LOS ANGELES • AMSTERDAM
SYDNEY • HAMBURG • PARIS • STOCKHOLM • ATHENS • TOKYO

Harlequin Presents edition published August 1981
ISBN 0-373-10448-0

Original hardcover edition published in 1981
by Mills & Boon Limited

CHAPTER ONE

Dusk was falling as Deborah walked out of the hotel. The hall porter rushed to open the door for her, giving her that flattering Latin smile which is always so oddly impersonal since it is bestowed on every female who passes, irrespective of age or appearance.

"You won't forget dinner is at eight, miss?" He spoke English with the faintest of American accents and was so used to speaking it that he no longer even looked proud of his fluency.

"I won't," she agreed. She was quite hungry, in fact, having refused all the plastic airport food she had been offered en route. She had not eaten since a light breakfast in London so many hours ago that she had lost count of time.

Her mind had been too busy with other thoughts. Someone once said that nothing so concentrates the mind as the prospect of being hanged in the morning, but pain can be equally absorbing. It leaves no room for anything else. The whole being becomes attentive to it, shutting out the rest of the world. Pulsing with that rhythm, Deborah had crossed Europe as if she were deaf, dumb, blind. Her invisible companion had never left her for a second, beating in her blood and making her nerves flicker with angry fire.

Her body's weariness had broken up that long vigil with pain now. She was aching from head to foot. Too much sitting around in airports and planes, too much noise and movement, had made her long to walk fast and alone, as though that would shake off her mood.

The hotel was on one of the back canals of Venice and when she walked out of it she found herself on the narrow *riva* which bordered the water, giving a footway for pedestrians. It was deserted. The back walls of other buildings stared blankly at her across the oily dark water. A bridge arched at the far end of the *riva*, framing further blank walls in an echoing perspective which ended in one of the pale evening mists which creep in from the lagoon.

There was something eerie about it. Deborah stood listening to the silence and it settled on her spirits like the mist. Behind her the hotel was quiet but well lit. The hall porter's face swam behind the glass door. He stared at her and she sensed he was about to come out to ask if she wanted directions. She walked away before he could.

Crossing the short bridge, she paused to look down into the canal. The water moved sluggishly and had a dank smell that reminded her of the Thames on winter evenings. Sometimes when they were going to see a play and had time to kill she and Robert had walked beside it, watching the round yellow globes of the Victorian lamps reflected on the water.

Laughing, she thought. Robert always made her laugh and she had had no premonition then that he would one day hurt her more than she could bear. It was just as well that human beings had no visions of the future. Today is always safer than tomorrow. Sufficient unto the day is the evil thereof, she told herself, turning away from the canal.

She couldn't even tell herself that he had made any secret of his nature. "Don't take me seriously," he would say from time to time, always laughing, and he had used the phrase so lightly that she had not even taken his warning seriously. She had gone on blithely falling in love, ignoring the danger signals. Robert was charming, he charmed without intention, the allure of his smile as meaningless as that flattering Latin smile the hall porter had given her. He enjoyed her company and for three months they had been constant companions. Deborah had a lively mind herself, a strong sense of humour, a good deal of intelligence.

Her sense of humour deserted her when she discovered that Robert was seeing someone else.

"I told you not to take me seriously," he said, faintly aggrieved. "We're friends, aren't we?"

"Friends?" The word had taken her breath away.

Robert had flushed slightly. The tone of her voice had conjured up memories which lay between them and which he could not deny, but he had said flatly: "Deb, I never promised you any commitment—you can't say I did. Don't try to build walls round me, I don't like it. I get claustrophobic when I feel people trying to claim exclusive rights."

She was grateful now that she had retained sufficient pride to hide the blow he had dealt her. At the time all she had thought about was getting away to ride the pain somehow where no one could watch. That was when she decided to take a holiday.

"At this time of year?" Andrea had asked, and there had been slight resentment in her voice.

Andrea loved her husband and her children, but she felt free to regard her sister's freedom from such ties with a disgruntled eye.

"You're always going abroad. You've just come back from Geneva. What do you need a holiday for?" Andrea had not waited to be told. She had launched into a catalogue of all the reasons why she needed a holiday a damned sight more than Deborah did, and once Andrea had begun one of her exhaustive lists of complaint there was no stopping her. Deborah had stopped listening after the first few seconds. There was no need to, anyway. Andrea's life was an open book to her; Andrea recited it freely every time they met.

Andrea was four years older and that fact dominated their relationship. The habit of seniority never left her. She scolded, bullied, brooded in exactly the way she had when they were children.

"You ought to get married," she ended up, breaking into Deborah's wrestling with pain and making her laugh in a harsh, unamused fashion.

"Thanks for the advice!"

Andrea had stared, half offended, half curious. "Is anything wrong?"

"I'm tired, that's all." Deborah had no intention of telling Andrea about Robert. Andrea had met him a number of times and been made half jealous, half satisfied, by her sister's choice. Robert was very presentable, far better looking than Tom, Andrea's husband, and Andrea had been torn between relief that it looked as if Deborah were going to get married at last and a feeling that it wasn't fair that she should come up with someone as attractive as that.

"You're tired? Don't make me laugh!" Andrea was always tired, she had been informed. "You try getting up at six with the baby and then having to get breakfast for Tom and the others, doing the housework..." The list had begun again. Andrea's life was narrow and busy and entirely fascinating to her. She imagined it must fascinate Deborah, too.

Everything has to end some time, even pain, Deborah reminded herself, walking without thinking into the blind wall of mist which had fallen in the narrow alleys. The dead sound of her own steps was the only sound she could hear. She paused, shivering, suddenly cold. Where was she?

She had walked without noticing. She had better retrace her steps. Turning, she walked back, the click of her heels ringing back from the high, windowless walls on either side and sinking into the waters of the canal without a trace.

They came out of the mist, softly, moving on rubber-heeled gym shoes. Deborah only had time to notice them before they were on either side of her, parting as if to let her through but their steps slowing. She glanced at them, feeling uneasy somehow. They were boys, thin and tall, in jeans and black sweaters, their long smooth faces not smiling yet with the ghost of amusement about them which they were not sharing with her but with each other, a silent exchange of looks across her which disturbed her.

She hastily looked away and began to quicken her step. They moved simultaneously, sandwiching her between them. She heard silent laughter. They did not make a sound, yet their shoulders, touching hers, shook with it.

In the silent, strange, misty streets Deborah felt lost and very much alone, and that increased the sense of panic which swept into her.

If they had spoken it would not have been so frightening. It was their silence which made their effect so hard for her to treat casually. They were no more than sixteen, she thought, but they were acting in a peculiar unison as though they had worked out what they would do before they came up with her. Had they been following her? Or had they done this before?

One of them ran his hand down her hip and Deborah's temper flared. She swung round towards him, thrusting him away, heat running into her face, then began to run, only to be trapped by them again, her arms held tightly. She screamed, and the sound of her voice bounced and echoed all around in the mist. One of them clapped a hand over her mouth, but from somewhere in the dark, dripping silence came another voice.

"What's wrong?" It was male and it was English, deep and surprised.

The boys didn't move and Deborah could not utter a sound, the hand over her mouth suffocated her. She made muffled, angry gasps instead.

"Where are you?"

There were footsteps and they were coming closer. She could not see the two boys now. They stood, tense and listening, reluctant to end their game but not wishing to get caught. Suddenly they thrust her away and ran silently, the faint rasp of rubber on stone the only evidence that they had ever been there. The mist swallowed them.

Deborah was trembling, swearing under her breath. She put out her hand and leaned on a wall. Her legs felt strangely weak and there was a damp perspiration that made her blouse stick to her spine.

The mist parted and a man came through it, the solid weight of his body displacing it. Breathing unevenly, Deborah stared at him.

"Was that you screaming? Why the hell didn't you answer? What was wrong? Lost, were you?"

Deborah couldn't find a word to say. She could hear her heart beating like an overwound watch.

"Are you all right?" He looked as if he wanted to hit her. He had an air of impatience. She felt he was going somewhere and in a hurry and displeased because she had delayed him. He wanted to deal with the problem of her and get away. "Say something, can't you?" he added, moving closer.

"Some boys jumped me," she said, and saw his eyebrows rise.

He looked around. "Boys?"

"They ran when you shouted back."

He did not look as if he believed a word of it. "I see," he said, considering her. "You aren't hurt?"

She shook her head. Now that she was safe and her heart was beginning to slow down she was embarrassed by the whole affair. She was flushed and irritable.

"I'm sorry you were troubled," she said.

He looked amused at the phrase. "I wasn't troubled," he said. "I thought you were someone lost in the mist."

"Yes, I am," she said. "Where am I?"

"I thought you were lost," he said, and she could tell he believed she had invented the story about the boys because she didn't want to admit she was lost and afraid. "This is the Loretsi canal. Where are you making for?"

"I want the Loretsi Hotel."

"It's a few hundred yards away, that's all." He began to smile and that annoyed her. "So you weren't lost, you just thought you were. You shouldn't have come out in this mist."

Deborah was in no mood to take patronising advice from any man. She bristled like a porcupine, her teeth on edge.

"Thank you," she flung like an insult at him, turning to walk away.

"I'll walk with you," he told her, falling into step without haste, his long legs keeping up with her easily. "In case you meet any more dangerous boys." The mockery was out in the open with that dig, his sideways look teasing her.

She didn't bother to insist on the reality of her attackers. She didn't care whether he believed her or not. The whole incident had left her shaken; the silent, hostile, menacing presence of those boys still lingered somewhere inside her.

She shivered and the man gave her a quick look. "You should have worn something warmer than that jacket," he told her. "It's October, remember. It can be quite chilly in Venice in the autumn."

The lights of the hotel cut through the mist. They halted outside it and Deborah began a polite sentence of thanks which was cut short by his smile and dismissive wave.

"Not at all. Glad to help. Are you staying here?"

"Yes."

"It's a good hotel, quiet and well run. The food's excellent."

"You know it well?" She wondered if he lived in Venice. He didn't somehow look like a tourist, and he sounded as though he knew Venice intimately.

In the light from the hotel Deborah was able to see him properly for the first time. He was a good head taller than herself, his shoulders wide and powerful, his body lean and tapering, the physique of an athlete. His face was striking without being handsome, those mobile brows set over dark blue eyes which watched her with faint amusement, his nose faintly arrogant in cast, his mouth relaxed and warm.

"I've stayed here," he admitted. "When did you arrive?"

"An hour or two ago."

He laughed. "And rushed out to explore at once? Not very wise in this weather."

"No." She was bristling again and from the way he watched her she sensed he knew it and was amused by it. She had the impression that he was a man often amused. His mouth had tiny lines radiating from it as though he often smiled. His skin was slightly bronzed. Had he just come back from some sunny holiday?

"Well, thank you again," she said, moving.

The hall porter was already opening the door. Deborah caught the look he gave the other man, the ready polite smile, but did not look back. She passed

into the hotel with waves of white mist and the door
closed behind her. The foyer was very warm, centrally
heated. Her body gratefully noted the warmth. She was
shivering and the porter said with concern: "A bad
evening, miss. We get these mists at this time of year."

She smiled and nodded. "I'm hungry," she told him.
There was a faint smell of food floating from the
dining-room and her stomach began to clamour at the
scent. "I'll go up and wash first."

She ate local dishes, the famous Venetian liver with
onions, which disguised the strong flavour of liver with
cream and herbs, and *zabaglione*, a light, frothy sweet
made with wine and eggs and cream. There were only a
few guests, a mere sprinkling of people at the other
tables, and they all stared curiously at her when she
entered, as though new guests were a matter of great interest to them.

Her waiter was very attentive, watching for every
movement, so that she had barely finished one course
before he was hovering to remove her plate.

He liked her hair. Italians always noticed blondes.
They were attracted by the Nordic colouring. The
waiter's dark eyes strayed over her all the time, smiling.
Deborah found it irritating. Once she might have been
flattered, amused. She would have enjoyed all the
masculine admiration. But at this present moment she
felt only one thing towards men: hostility. She found
male admiration almost insulting tonight. Stop staring,
she wanted to snap at him, and her green eyes said
something of the sort when she looked up once to find
those soulful eyes fixed on her. Deborah glared and the
waiter shuffled away on his tired, waiter's feet, his

shoulders crestfallen, so that she felt stupidly guilty because he was not a young man and his admiration was purely artistic. There had not been the vaguest hint of a pass in his stare.

She sat for some time drinking coffee, wishing it was not Italian, because she wasn't fond of their coffee. She preferred her coffee strong and rich and the bland, milky flavour was dull. The waiter came back and she asked if there were any liqueurs. He cheered up at this and rushed off to get her a Drambuie, pouring it for her into her next coffee in a grandiloquent ritualistic way, as though she had asked for it just to please him, which, in a sense, she had. She sipped and smiled at him and he glowed with delight before he vanished again.

It improved the coffee, anyway. Deborah yawned, her hand over her mouth, feeling dull and sleepy now. The food had a soporific effect. It was the effect of the journey, really. She had been moving all day, on her way, going somewhere, and that was what she had wanted. To be at rest was to think of Robert, and she hadn't wanted to do that, although he had been in her mind all day, nevertheless. She hadn't been able to cry with people all round her, though. That was what she had thought. She would have to keep a bright face, look ordinary. So she had fled across Europe to escape pain and taken it with her like an invisible companion.

The hall porter was just going off duty. "Sleep well, miss," he said as she passed, and the man replacing him gave her a toothy smile and a bow as he handed her her room key.

She ordered rolls and coffee for breakfast in her room. "And a newspaper?" she was asked.

"*The Times*," she said, because that was usually the only English paper one could be sure of getting abroad. The others often arrived much too late for breakfast.

As she turned away she bumped into someone. He steadied her with both hands on her arms. Deborah glanced up, a polite smile ready, but it withered on her mouth.

"Feeling better?"

"Thank you, yes." She couldn't pretend to be pleased to see him. He reminded her of the panic and fear she had half forgotten. And she increasingly didn't like the amusement in his blue eyes.

She was moving away as he said: "No bad dreams, I hope." He was laughing, but Deborah wasn't. She knew she was going to have bad dreams. Get lost, she wanted to say, and every line of her body said it for her as she carefully did not look back at him.

The hotel had one of those old-fashioned lifts with wrought iron cages painted gilt. The curling, baroque patterns gave one a view of the whole foyer as the lift rose and one looked down through the open ironwork. Deborah looked down and felt a sting of pure rage as she saw the tall, dark-haired man watching her from below. He was eyeing her legs with a thoughtful appraisal. His glance lifted and she glared at him, briefly, before she went out of sight.

There were flowers on the table in her room. She paused to smell their faint scent and caught a glimpse of herself in the mirror behind them. Her face was flushed and her eyes had a hard sheen to them. She looked belligerent, ready to do battle with someone. It was some improvement on the grey misery in which she had been sunk for days. It would close in on her again, like the Venetian mist, but for the moment she was alive, awake.

The flowers had the forgettable, plastic perfection of hothouse blooms. Robert had once sent her red roses like this—long-stemmed, exquisite blooms which yet seemed unreal. "Beautiful," she had told him, because she had wanted to please him, but she would have preferred a bunch of violets bought from a basket of squashed flowers in the street. Robert was a man of impulse. He did things without reckoning the cost, for himself or anyone else. He liked to live at random, rushing after anything that caught his eye. "Don't take me seriously." Robert refused to take life itself seriously and Deborah once thought that admirable, but now she saw it very differently.

It was all a question of point of view. The place where you are standing dictates what you see and how you see it.

She lay in the bed, trying to sleep, watching mist drift about the room like a homeless ghost. The sound of water lapping crumbling stone steps came from the canal beyond the window. She had a little balcony outside her room. "Don't walk on it, please," the porter had urged. "It is not safe." She had waited until he had gone and then she had opened the french windows and stepped out on to the unsafe balcony. The smell of the canal had been stronger then; it always smelt strongly during the hours of sunlight. The wall opposite had a few tiny windows in it all of which were barred as though to stop the people inside from leaping out into the canal. Was it a hotel? Or a prison, perhaps? Or a convent which had to guard against escaping nuns? She had stared at the windows, expecting to see sad faces behind them, but they had given no clues.

It wasn't as though Robert was the first man she had ever been in love with—she knew love could go as lightly as it had come. She was twenty-seven now. She had been nineteen the first time she fell in love. Before that she had tried love on like a possible hat, yet always in fun, playing at it. When she did fall in love at last that had been fun, too, except that one day the fun had drained out of it and the young man who had seemed a mixture of Adonis and Robert Redford had come into focus as himself, a boy of twenty with a quick temper and a liking for his own way. Deborah couldn't even remember what he looked like.

Would she one day not remember what Robert looked like? She shut her eyes and tried to forget it now. It wasn't so much his looks as the way he smiled, the sound of his voice, that feeling of delight which the lover can experience at the mere fact of someone else.

He didn't make a fool of me, Deborah told herself; I made a fool of myself. I'm good at that. It's probably my chief talent.

"You never listen properly," her boss had told her once. She had been a young reporter then, running on tiptoe to get experience of life and work, never stopping to hear what anyone told her in case she missed life round the corner.

She had made a stupid mistake, confusing two names. Two irate and very important men had converged on the newsroom to protest about her. "You never listen properly."

She should have listened when Robert told her: "Don't take me seriously."

He had been honest. He hadn't asked her to fall in love with that depth and intensity.

They had met at an official luncheon. Deborah had been there to accept an award on behalf of her news team for their coverage of a bitter little war in one of the emerging African countries. Western interest had been brief. A few news stories, pictures, and then the subject had faded from the newspapers. Deborah had been angry while she listened to the self-congratulatory speeches. She had just flown back from seeing things she knew she would never forget and the whole thing had seemed unreal to her—the expensive food, the men in well-tailored suits, the cigars and wine. She couldn't help remembering a starving child who had begged in the streets of a township for food. She hadn't had any to give and so she had poured all her loose change into the little boy's hands. She had been on her way to fly home. The memory of his emaciated face had gone with her every mile of the way.

But she wasn't there to give her opinions. She had made her polite little speech of thanks, and to sink the memory she had drunk more than she normally did. A mixture of wine and anger had made her sparkle. Robert had sat next to her. They fell into light talk and as the lunch ended he asked her: "May I see you again?"

At first she was so often away doing a story that it was some time before she realised how involved she was getting, but she had thought it was mutual. Robert was always so happy to see her, so regretful when she had to fly off again.

He lived and worked in London. London was his idea of heaven. He knew everyone and went everywhere. As editor of a well-read magazine he got masses of invitations and was always welcome.

Robert was a social creature, he liked good company and his tastes were all gregarious ones. He got complimentary tickets for every new play, opera, ballet. He got party invitations by the bag. Apart from his importance as an influential editor he made a charming guest. He was popular, especially with women.

Deborah had realised from the start that he had an eventful past. She got used to finding herself facing someone from it—a woman with curious, amused eyes who half wanted to swap anecdotes about him and half wanted to keep them jealously to herself. Robert was always delighted to meet them. He never showed any sign of embarrassment or confusion. "Marvellous to see you again," he would assure them.

Deborah had been through a phase of being sorry for them, the women who hadn't been able to hold him, not realising that it would be her turn very soon to recognise that you couldn't hold Robert. He wouldn't let you.

She knew that now; she wished she had realised it from the start. She wouldn't have this sharp, niggling pain in her chest, like a mouse imprisoned by her rib-cage, gnawing its way out.

The fact that love was an illusion didn't help at the moment. The illusion of love still clung to her. When it faded, the pain would go too, she told herself. She wished she had rather more wine with her dinner. Sleep was being evasive.

She closed her eyes and lay very still, breathing regularly, inviting sleep to come.

When she opened them again it was daylight. The mist had lifted. A frail sunlight was fingering its way across the walls in a nervous fashion and there was a sound of voices on the narrow *riva* outside the hotel.

It was a moment before she realised that what had woken her was the tap at the door. It came again and she called sleepily: "Come in."

Her breakfast had arrived. No *Times*, though. The sallow-skinned floor maid explained with a shrug: "No papers—the mist."

Deborah made no comment. She slipped into her loose blue silk negligee and sat up, pouring coffee and spreading a roll with butter and thick cherry jam.

The coffee was milky flavoured again. What did they make it with? Acorns?

When she had finished she showered and dressed in a cream trouser suit. She meant to take another walk and send some postcards. "Send us a postcard," Andrea had ordered, not so much for the sake of hearing from her as because the eldest of Andrea's children, Kerry, collected stamps and Deborah had given his collection a wide selection from the places she visited. She never forgot to send him a card even when she was only somewhere for a day or two. Kerry was seven and believed the world revolved around him. He was at the age when this seemed an obvious fact and it wouldn't occur to him that Deborah, his favourite aunt, could fail to remember him. Deborah would hate to hurt his feelings or puncture his ego at such a tender age.

At intervals in her busy life she sometimes thought

how nice it would be to have a son like Kerry. She was
fond of him. "Easy for you," Andrea would tell her if
she said so. "You only see him on his best behaviour.
You should be here when he's got measles or doesn't
want to go to bed because there's something on TV he
wants to see. He's a little monster then."

Perhaps the grass was always greener on the other
side of a fence. She envied Andrea who, for all her complaints, was busy and needed and knew it. Andrea envied her the glamour and excitement she imagined
Deborah enjoyed.

Having bought a selection of postcards she wandered
into a street café and ordered a coffee which she sipped
as she wrote brief messages on the cards. For the first
time in months she did not send one to Robert, an omission of which she was deeply conscious.

Shuffling the cards together, she was about to get up
when she saw the man from the hotel. He did not notice
her; he was crossing the wide, pigeon-infested square
with a woman. Deborah watched them, her expression
wry. That dark head was bent as he listened to what his
companion was saying. She walked quickly to keep up
with the stride of those long legs, her very high heels
clicking.

He smiled suddenly, his face filled with humour and
charm. Deborah felt again the hostility she had felt last
night when she caught him inspecting her legs, especially
as she saw the responsive smile he got from his companion. She knew that sort of smile; Robert shed them
casually on everyone he met.

She looked away, walking in the opposite direction,
and found a vaporetto to take her back to her own

canal. Today the air had that calm, lucid quality which enriches Venice and garnishes the decaying splendour of the palaces and old churches. The mist might never have come down. A light breeze blew along the Grand Canal, rippling the surface and breaking it into a million tiny dancing fractions of light.

A child in a passing gondola, eating a huge strawberry icecream cone, leaned over too far and dropped her icecream into the canal, and the shriek of fury made everyone start to laugh. Deborah's spirits lifted. She looked at the pink and gold stucco of passing façades and felt happy. It was a brief impulse of happiness, but it was a hand stretched from the future, reminding her that even grief doesn't last for ever. One day she would be free of pain again.

Going into the hotel she surprised the porter with a real smile. "A good morning, miss?" He looked as though that pleased him, as though Venice belonged to him and he had been resenting the fact that she was obviously not happy there. Now he was delighted.

"Very good," she said, although nothing had happened, except that the sun had shone and a child had dropped her icecream into the canal.

As the lift started with a reluctant jerk she saw the dark-haired man crossing the foyer. Their eyes met. Deborah almost smiled at him, too, but at the last moment she looked away. It was safer.

CHAPTER TWO

WHEN Deborah went down to dinner that evening the lift wasn't working. A printed card had been hung on the gate. Under repair, it announced. That meant she would have to walk down four flights of stairs and up again later. They wouldn't be repairing it tonight.

The stairs were marble, ornate and well worn. Her feet made little clacking noises on every one. So far she had somehow got the impression that the hotel was only half full. One rarely saw other guests moving about, and Deborah was rather glad about that. The staff had more time and were in a better temper.

On the first floor a door stood open. As she passed someone came out if it, jingling a key on one finger. Deborah gave him a polite half smile which died as she recognised him.

He had recognised her, too. "Had a good day?" he asked, catching up with her.

"Yes, thank you." He reminded her of her own panic the night before and she was not over-pleased to see him.

He looked different tonight. She got the feeling he was angry about something. His bones were tight under the smooth brown skin and his eyes had a hard light in them. He looked rather formidable in that mood.

Deborah was relieved he hadn't looked like that when he came out of the mist.

His blue eyes shot over her and suddenly changed. "Doing anything tonight?"

She stiffened. "Eating dinner and getting an early night," she told him, already pricking at what she sensed was coming.

"I saved your life last night," he murmured, half mocking. "Or worse, depending on what your little boys had in mind."

"I had the feeling you didn't believe in them."

"Implicitly." He was mocking her again. "Anyway, don't you think you owe me a small favour?"

"I'll do the same for you if ever you get waylaid by teenage girls," she promised.

"That's precisely what I had in mind."

Deborah stared blankly.

"I've got to go to a party tonight. There's no way I can avoid it without offending someone I can't afford to offend, but if I go alone I'm going to find myself under attack by a thick-skinned, persistent young lady who doesn't seem to understand polite negatives."

"Try some impolite ones."

He laughed. "Her father is the chap I can't afford to offend."

"You have got problems," she shrugged.

"I'd be very grateful if you could act bodyguard for one evening."

Deborah gave him a cool stare. "Try an escort agency."

"A bit late for that," he said. "I had a date laid on,

but she just rang up to say she had a migraine. I dare not go alone.''

"Oh, is it that sort of party? Not my scene, then, I'm afraid.'' She gave him a polite little smile and then, as they had arrived at the dining-room, walked away to her own table. The dark-haired man joined her without being invited, seating himself as casually as though he was sure of his welcome.

"Oh, it's a very formal, dull sort of party," he assured her. "Teresa is the only problem. She's spoilt and for some reason she has her sights set on me. If I'm alone she'll cling to me like glue.''

The waiter divided his tired smile between them, handing each a dinner menu. Deborah looked across the table with irritation at her unwanted companion.

"The liver's good," he told her, apparently oblivious of her meaningful stare.

"I know. I had it last night," she snapped.

"Try the veal," he suggested.

Deborah turned her frustrated wrath towards the menu, decided on chicken and ordered briskly. "*Pollo Principessa—si, signorina,*" the waiter smiled before turning to the other guest at the table.

When he had given his own order and the waiter had gone, the dark-haired man surveyed her with a thoughtful face. "My name is Matthew," he informed her, waiting for her to reply so decisively that she found herself doing so with an ill grace.

"Deborah." He hadn't given a surname, so neither did she.

"In Venice on holiday?" he asked and went on, "Where are you from?"

"London," Deborah said curtly, wishing she dared ask him to go and sit elsewhere but not quite having the nerve with those blue eyes on her.

"Talking of London, what do you do for a living?" He ran those experienced blue eyes down her. "A model?"

She knew that that was carefully delivered flattery and her glance told him so. "No," she said, not telling him what she did do.

"Talkative little soul, aren't you?"

"I'm here for some peace and quiet," Deborah informed him, staring at him pointedly.

"I'm here to sign an important business deal, but if I quarrel with Teresa it may well get loused up."

"I'm quite sure you're capable of dealing tactfully with a lovesick teenager." He looked more than capable of it. She did not believe this sob story about the little Teresa.

"I told you, she's very persistant."

"I'm sorry, but it's hardly my problem." She did not believe a word he said. He was spinning a line and she wasn't falling for it. A year ago, she might well have pretended to believe him and gone to this party, because he was a very attractive man and she was by no means blind to his attraction, but he had caught her at the wrong moment and she didn't want to know.

"No man is an island," he said in that deep, amused voice.

"Trite but true."

"I did you a good turn," he reminded her. "Next time I hear you screaming in the mist, do you want me to walk the other way?"

"There won't be a next time. I learn quickly." That

was true, she thought. Robert had taught her a lesson, and she wasn't going to forget that one in a hurry.

"What did you say you did for a living? You're very hard-hearted."

"I didn't." She had often found that it paid not to tell people you were a journalist. They either plunged into endless stories they thought would look good in the newspaper or ran white-faced in the opposite direction because they thought she might be trying to get the inside story of their lives. Feeling him staring at her, she smiled sweetly and pointed out: "Neither did you. What do you do?"

"I'm a businessman."

"That covers a multitude of sins."

He laughed. "Now what makes me feel you don't much like businessmen?"

The waiter arrived. Deborah concentrated on her melon and Parma ham. She hadn't ordered any wine, but found her glass being filled. Matthew gave her a wicked grin.

"How kind," Deborah said with an insincere smile.

His dark hair was very thick and vital-looking, free from any sign of grey, brushed back from his face but constantly straying so that he had to push it away with an impatient hand. His movements had an air of restless energy about them. From his build he was an active man and she imagined he found it hard to stay still for long.

"Is there someone who might object if you went to the party?" he asked, giving her hands a thoughtful glance which observed the lack of rings on her left hand.

"Yes," she nodded.

"Ah," he said. "A lover?"

"No, me."

He laughed again. "Is your hair naturally that colour?" he asked, surprising her.

She looked up, swallowing a piece of melon and coughing as it went down the wrong way. "Yes, it is," she spluttered, then caught his eye and knew he had deliberately been teasing her. "Very funny!"

"You should wear it longer. It would suit you."

"It's easier to deal with at this length."

"What a practical girl," he mocked. The waiter removed their first course and served the second, delicately spooning beurre noisette over Matthew's veal, his expression priestlike. He took his job seriously, one could see.

Deborah had intended to hurry up with her meal and get away before Matthew managed to talk her into this party, but the wine was making her relax and softening her mood. It was very good wine and very expensive, she imagined, trying to read the label upside down but defeated by the white damask napkin covering it. The waiter replaced it in the ice bucket and went. She looked at Matthew, who calmly told her the vintage and year.

"I wondered what it was," she admitted.

"I know you did. I noticed."

"It's very good."

"Isn't it?" He looked at her meal. "That looks good, too. I told you the food here was exceptional. The chef is Paris-trained and has been here for years. I always stay here when I'm in Venice."

"You don't live here, then?"

He looked surprised. "No, I live in London, like you."

"But you're often in Venice?"

"From time to time," he agreed. Some new arrivals passed the table and Matthew glanced sideways to admire the figure of one of them, his blue eyes sliding from her face to her slender legs. When he looked back, Deborah gave him a sardonic smile.

"Why don't you ask *her*?" she suggested.

"We haven't been introduced."

"That shouldn't stop you. I don't recall being introduced to you myself."

"Ah, but you owe me a favour."

"Remind me never to ask you for help again."

"The boot is on the other foot." He threw her a carefully appealing smile. "An hour at the party wouldn't hurt you, would it?"

Deborah shrugged, sipping some more wine. She felt impervious and oddly lighthearted. A party might be fun, particularly as she wouldn't know anyone and need not exert herself to be cheerful. The wine was circulating in her veins and giving the world a more agreeable colour.

Matthew scented victory. He leaned forward, his blue eyes coaxing. "Yes?"

"I'll think about it."

He looked very please with himself. "Have you been to Venice before?" That was clever, she thought, changing the subject like that. This man would bear watching. He knew when to lift pressure.

"Yes."

"You like it, then? Or you wouldn't come again."

"You do like stating the obvious, don't you?"

His look measured her with cool appraisal. "And you like slapping people down."

"That depends."

"On what?"

"On whether they deserve it."

"What was he like?" he asked suddenly.

Deborah's hand froze on its way to her lips and she put down the fork. Staring at it, she asked casually: "What? Who are we talking about?"

"The chap whose punishment I'm taking."

She shot him a look. "Clever!"

"As you say, I like stating the obvious." His lips were wry, the blue eyes intelligent. "Recent, was it?"

"Your veal is getting cold." She continued with her meal and after a moment so did he. They didn't say anything for several moments and it was not until after they had started on the orange water ice they had both chosen as a dessert that Matthew spoke again.

"How old are you?"

Deborah laughed abruptly. "You do ask personal questions!"

"I wondered how you'd managed to get to around... what? twenty-five or six... without learning how to take hard knocks lightly."

She flushed a little. "I'm twenty-seven, actually, but maybe the guesswork was deliberately tactful."

"No comment otherwise?"

"About hard knocks? No, I don't think so. I'm not in the habit of discussing my private life with strangers."

"Very wise, I've no doubt. Neither am I, not that it seems to stop people discussing it, in my experience."

"No, it rarely does," she agreed. Andrea would discuss avidly every corner of Deborah's private life, given half a chance. She didn't know about Robert yet, but when she did Deborah winced at the thought of the probing questions, the heavy sympathy, the half-irritated advice she was going to get. Andrea, of course, would think Deborah had somehow scared Robert off. Deborah was aware that her sister loved her in an impatient, half reluctant way, but it was a fondness which reserved the right to blame Deborah for what happened to her, as though she invited it.

"Especially journalists," Matthew muttered, his face frowning.

Deborah looked at him sharply. "What?"

"Journalists," he repeated, not catching the note in her voice. "I detest them. They invent what they don't know and get what they're told wrong."

Deborah put a spoonful of orange water ice in her mouth. It melted slowly on her tongue and gave her a good excuse for not saying a word.

After a moment she said casually: "Do you have much trouble with journalists?" and made it sound light and amused, disbelieving.

Matthew's frown broke up and he grinned at her. "You wouldn't believe the trouble I've seen."

"Try me," Deborah offered, wide-eyed and smiling.

Who was she dining with? Matthew something, she thought. And not short of a pound or two, judging by the wine they were drinking. He hadn't told her his surname and now she suspected that that had been due to ulterior motives. He hadn't wanted her to know who he was. So who was he?

"The *paparazzi*, for a start," he said. "They'll do. Sharks and vultures, all of them. They chase you round the city, scenting blood—Italy's worst aspect."

Italy had a name for that, it was true. The freelance

photographers and reporters who made a living by following well-known names to get a story were internationally famous. They didn't follow people like vultures waiting for a death if their prey was not a big name, though. Matthew, she thought, searching for a famous name beginning with it.

She couldn't ask him now without arousing his curiosity. She would have to wait for clues. Sooner or later she would find out. The hotel porter would tell her, no doubt.

The coffee arrived, but tonight it was much better. Matthew had ordered liqueurs with it and had cream floating in thick islands on the top.

Deborah was flushed and relaxed now, but under the smiling face her mind was working at top speed.

"You are coming to the party?" Matthew asked, and got a dazzling smile.

"I'd love to come!"

He look surprised, but not astonished, no doubt imagining that it was the effect of the good wine he had been pouring into her which had changed her mind. Deborah looked meltingly at him as she drank her coffee.

It wouldn't be a bad idea, she had realised. When she asked for time off, her editor had loomed over her, scowling. "You've had your days off for this quarter. What do you think this is! A charity?"

"I'd be very grateful, Hal," she had said, looking away from him.

He had caught something of her grey misery and fallen silent. He was a large, aggressive man with a very loud voice which could be heard from one end of the building to the other at times. He was also a man with quick intuition and an unintrusive sense of occasion. He didn't know what this was all about, but he didn't want to know. He merely saw that Deborah needed to get away. His great shoulders had shrugged.

"Okay. I'll expect a favour in return some day. You can have a week."

"Ten days, if you could manage that," she had said.

"Have a pint of my blood, why don't you," he had muttered, walking away.

He would be pleased if she brought back a story of some kind. It would justify him for his kindness to her.

Deborah was a member of a small, hand-picked team of writers who dealt almost entirely with foreign stories. They had a bag packed ready to fly off at a moment's notice. Often they all went, en masse, when a story was big enough to warrant saturation coverage, but sometimes they went alone to cover some particular situation. Deborah was the only female member of the team. She had to work twice as hard as the men because any mistake she made was always put down to her sex and magnified. "What can you expect? She's a woman," one of the others would say, half joking, but always half serious.

Her job fascinated her, kept her at full stretch, so that she hadn't noticed the years slipping past without the thought of marriage ever cropping up. Andrea had pointed it out to her once or twice. "It's your job," she had said. "You never have time for anything else." She was right, although Deborah hadn't bothered to admit as much. She didn't need to, anyway. Andrea was always right, in Andrea's opinion. She didn't wait to have her opinions confirmed. She stated them with dogmatic assurance and then swept on to state some more.

"It's a dressy affair," said Matthew, and she started, looking at him blankly.

"What is?"

"The party." He smiled, his eyes creasing in amusement. "Miles away, weren't you? Have you got a pretty party dress on you?" She could see that that hadn't occurred to him until now and he looked slightly concerned.

"I think I can find something suitable." Her tone was dry and he grinned back at her.

"I had a feeling you might. Are you sure you aren't a model? That's definitely a model girl figure you've got there."

"I'm just skinny."

"Not from where I'm sitting."

She was rather too thin, Andrea had often told her. Too many rushed or skimpy meals, too much dashing about and late hours, Andrea usually went on. She disapproved of Deborah's life style and envied it all in the same breath.

Their mother had died when Deborah was fifteen and their father had left the care of Deborah to Andrea. He was a merchant seaman, the captain of a ship freighting between London and Stockholm, and he had no idea how to look after two young girls. Andrea's mixture of fondness and scolding had grown up during those years.

Matthew walked up the stairs with her, paused outside his own room and asked: "How long will it take you to get ready?"

"A quarter of an hour," she promised.

He looked disbelieving. "If you say so."

Deborah was very used to changing her clothes at top

speed and she knew precisely how long it would take her. She smiled at him. "Fifteen minutes," she repeated, and left him.

She had only brought one suitable dress with her, and that had been by sheer chance. She hadn't expected to be going anywhere special, but it had been habit that made her take down the green dress. She always took something special for evening wear because in her experience you never knew what might come up and it paid to go prepared.

She showered, dressed and did her make-up with expert speed. In exactly fiteen minutes she was back at Matthew's door. He opened it to her brisk tap, his brows shooting up.

"Incredible!" he commented.

"That will teach you not to make snap judgments."

"In my experience women always underestimate the time it takes them to get ready."

"If there's one thing I can't stand it's men who make sweeping generalisations about women!" Deborah snapped.

"There's always an exception to every rule," he agreed, looking amused. He was in his shirt and was fiddling with his cuff-links in a desultory fashion.

"Aren't you ready yet?" Deborah looked at him with mockery.

"I plead guilty. I shan't be a second."

She took hold of his cufflink and slotted it deftly into the shirt. "Thank you," he said, laughing, then turned to pick up his black evening jacket.

He looked quite startlingly attractive in the evening suit. The formality of it suited him, emphasised the width of shoulder and length of leg. She could well imagine that an impressionable teenage girl might find him swooningly desirable. His relaxed and charming manner would no doubt seem the height of sophistication to the unknown Teresa.

Why did sophistication always seem so fascinating when one was young? Deborah could remember feeling the same herself. She felt a pang of sympathy for the girl.

The sympathy provoked a question. Had Matthew flirted lightly with the girl at first? Another Robert, she thought, watching his face as he slid his wristwatch over his hand.

"Ready," he said, looking up. His blue eyes flicked over her and glinted with appreciation. "Am I permitted to say that you look even more model-girl than ever in that dress?"

"Thank you," she said without warmth. She was not going to walk into another relationship. At the moment, men were on the banned list for her. He could go and waste his charm on someone else.

"You're a wary little fish, aren't you?" he murmured as he guided her out of the room, his eyes speculative as they darted sideways at her.

The hall porter got them a taxi. "A Venice special," Matthew pointed out as he helped her into the gondola.

"The only way to travel," Deborah agreed, settling luxuriously under the raised hood.

"I've ordered a moon, too," he informed her as he took the seat beside her and the gondola shot away from the landing stage.

There it was, hanging languidly in the deep purple sky. Deborah eyed it without favour.

"Venice moonlight is famous," said Matthew, his arm sliding along the back of her.

She shifted and his arm dropped away. He made no comment and she asked: "Where's the party?"

"A palazzo," Matthew told her. "It really is," catching her incredulous look. "Three hundred years old and slowly sinking into the mud but still worth seeing. Signor Scalatio has the whole of the ground floor. It's divided into apartments—they usually are these days. Too big for one person. This is a little palace—a damned great house, in fact, but they always prefer the more dignified name."

"Signor Scalatio is your Teresa's father?"

"She isn't mine." He sounded faintly irritated.

"But wants to be?"

Matthew turned his head and his dark blue eyes were hard. "I don't quite like the way you say that. I haven't given her an inch of encouragement, it's all in her own head."

There was no mist tonight. The city lay bathed in silvery moonlight, the dark waters spread with it, their surface calm and still. In this mysterious, unreal light the decay and shabbiness was not visible. The stucco gleamed gently as they floated past the palaces. Voices carried at night. The occupants of other gondolas whispered to each other and even if they were talking of prices, petrol, how to get a mortgage, somehow their lowered tones made their talk sound romantic.

Deborah did not like it. She felt a coldness on her skin and the ache in her chest intensified. She wanted to cry.

She had been through a succession of stages in her attitude to Robert over the last week. She hated him, despised him, hated herself and despised herself. She wanted to ring him and say anything, however trivial, just to hear his voice, but she had a stubborn streak and a lot of pride, and she hadn't done it. There is no bitterness quite as deep as that of unrequited love.

Hell hath no fury, she silently reminded herself, and smiled in a tight, angry way at the moonlight drifting with that silent eloquence over the city.

Was that what Robert had said to himself about her? It's all in her own head. She looked briefly at Matthew, who was watching the buildings slide past on the right-hand side. Although Robert had warned her: don't take me seriously, he had flirted with her, made a dead set at her, for months. If she had mistaken his intentions it was because Robert had made it easy for her to do that. Was that what Matthew had done to Teresa Scalatio?

If he wanted to sign a deal with her father he might well have used Teresa to help him. From the charm he expended on her, she could imagine that he would always smile at women like that, his eyes coaxing and inviting. Now that his deal was a settled thing he might be trying to ditch the girl. His intentions had never been serious, either.

He turned and their eyes met. She saw his face change, the calm expression go and a shrewd, probing enquiry come into the blue eyes. He had seen the hostility in her features and was wondering about it.

She forced the ghost of a smile. "Your moon was worth the money," she said.

"I'm glad you think so. I ordered it especially for you."

"How thoughtful!"

He smiled, but there was still that watchful fixity in his face. "What was he like?" he asked.

Her eyes flickered and moved away. "How far is it to the palazzo, did you say?"

"What went wrong? Did you quarrel with him? Or did it just all come to pieces in your hands?"

Deborah didn't answer that, either, and after a pause he went on quite gently: "Love's like toothache. It can be hell while it lasts, but once it's gone you wonder what all the fuss was about."

"You're an expert, are you?" She couldn't suppress the antagonism in her voice.

"I'm a human being. That makes me an expert; on love, at least. If I'd reached the age of thirty-six without knowing something about it I'd be a very cold fish."

"Which you're not," she said with a mocking little smile, disputing it.

His eyes began to gleam. He moved closer under the dark hood of the gondola, his arm back around her, resting along the ironwork of the seat. "Want some proof of that?"

"No, thank you," said Deborah, stiffening.

"Pity." He was laughing under his breath. "I'm always ready to give demonstrations."

"I'm sure." She looked pointedly at his arm and he removed it. The gondola bumped against the crumbling stone of a flight of steps. She had barely looked at the gondolier who stood behind them, his arm moving rhythmically as he sped through the water. Matthew helped her to alight and she went up the steps, feeling the shifting stone beneath her feet, slimy from the constant lap of water at the base. A beautiful ironwork lamp split golden light around her. She saw the mossy green surface of the stone by it, gleaming wet and slippery.

The palazzo was grey and blue, an arched balcony running along the front of it on the first floor, and looked as though a slight push would send it toppling into the canal. Time had eaten away the stone fretwork, the carvings and pilasters, so that it looked like a house under sentence of death.

"It must have been lovely once." Deborah thought it a sad place. It cried out to be saved from the waters, but it was so huge that it would cost a fortune even to have it painted or re-stuccoed, she imagined. It was settling slowly into ruin with a resigned air.

"There are about a dozen families living in it now. It's like a rabbit warren inside." Matthew had his hand under her elbow and was urging her towards the house.

The heavy front door stood partially open. Matthew glanced at the row of cards and bells beside it and put his finger on one of them. They heard feet approaching across a stone floor and then a girl appeared. She flung herself at Matthew, her face alight with happiness.

"Matt!" She burst into rapid Italian, her arms clinging round his neck, and Deborah, watching, felt her heart clench in sympathy. Poor little thing, she thought, then, angrily: what a swine he is!

CHAPTER THREE

"ENGLISH, please, Teresa, I've brought a friend with me." Matthew unlocked the girl's arms from his neck and detached her gently and without haste. "This is Deborah."

Teresa swivelled in a violent, jerky movement and looked at Deborah with undisguised dislike. *"Ciao"*, she said sulkily, her full lower lip stuck out in a frosty pout.

"Hallo," Deborah answered, not smiling, yet with a smile in her eyes which did not insist on a response but offered friendship if the girl cared to accept it.

Teresa did not care to, her face made that plain. Her face made all her emotions plain. She had not learnt to hide them and she had no wish to start learning. She was somewhere between seventeen and nineteen, Deborah judged. Small, rounded, very feminine, she had black hair which shone like polished silk and was curled lightly round her olive-skinned face. Her dark eyes were enormous and lustrous, fringed with delicate lashes which she fluttered with great effect as she looked back at Matthew.

She spoke in Italian again and he frowned at her, "Deborah doesn't speak Italian."

What made him so sure of that? Deborah thought, prickling.

She did, in fact, speak a little, but certainly not enough

to follow the spate of words Teresa was pouring out to him. It was essential for her job that Deborah had languages. She spoke French, German, Russian and Arabic with varying degrees of fluency and was currently learning Chinese. Her tutor was a tiny Chinese girl who worked in the newsroom as a secretary and who lived in the cramped rooms above her father's Chinese restaurant. Deborah had to fit her lessons in when she was in England and they were always interrupted by the lively antics of Chi's three brothers. The boys appeared to be boneless and threw themselves about the room like hoops, laughing at Chi's quick scolding. Deborah liked the warmth of the family atmosphere. Her lessons were fun, even if they had not yet got her very far with the extremely complicated Chinese language.

"Deborah is a friend of mine," Matthew was saying, and she had the feeling he had been saying it earlier in Italian. His voice had the ring of someone who has repeated something several times.

Teresa turned and walked away, her slim shoulders hunched sullenly. They followed her across the damp, chilly stone hall. The walls were an indistinguishable shade of off-white, the plaster flaking in long curls. Some of it drifted off as they passed and showered the stone floor with flecks of white.

There was music coming from an open door. Teresa went inside the apartment without looking back to see if they were coming.

Somehow, from the state of the building, Deborah had got the impression that the apartment would be equally shabby, but as she walked inside she realised with a shock how wrong she had been. It was both stylish and luxurious. The height of the rooms, their stately length and breadth, might have made them rather gloomy and bare, had they not been furnished and decorated in superb taste. The designer had broken up the room into living areas, using cascading plants, polished bronze-like statuary, low bookcases, to divide and yet to keep the space open and flowing. The eye swept round the enormous room and somehow the crowd of people in it were swallowed up easily by the grandeur of the surroundings.

People stood and talked, glasses in their hands, or sat on one of the symmetrically planned seating areas which were all one bland shade of cream, faintly Japanese in appearance with hard low cushions for arm and back rests. Great mirrors on the walls reflected back and forth, diminishing and enlarging.

A man detached himself from a group and came towards them, smiling. "Matthew, nice to see you!" He spoke English with a strong American accent, but his looks were entirely Italian and Deborah did not need to be told he was Teresa's father.

Matthew introduced her and she shook hands, getting a warm smile which yet had a thoughtful curiosity in it. Signor Scalatio looked over his shoulder at where his daughter was talking far too brightly to some of the other guests, and then he looked at Matthew, but Deborah could not read his thoughts in his dark eyes.

He was rather short, heavily built without being fat, his skin a darker olive than his daughter's smooth young skin had been, faintly heavier in texture, the closeness of his shave not quite erasing that shadow of stubble. His hair was thinning, especially above the brow, brushed flat and rather shiny under the roseate light.

"Deborah," he murmured, still holding her hand. "I like that—it suits you. You look like a Deborah."

"What does a Deborah look like?" she asked, making no effort to retrieve her hand and looking into his dark eyes, trying to uncover the thoughts he was hiding. What did he think of his daughter's determined pursuit of Matthew? Did he approve? Or disapprove?

"Like you," he returned, smiling. He had a fullness of lip which betrayed sensuality and enjoyment of life, his smile spontaneous and lively. She did not need to know anything about him to realise that he liked women. His liquid eyes were wandering over her without becoming offensive, offering an entirely friendly appreciation.

"Have you met many Deborahs?"

His smile deepened into laughter. "I think you are the first one." He glanced aside at Matthew who was listening with expressionless attention. "Your friend is charming." He spoke in Italian, but Deborah understood him, more by the context than anything else. "Very pretty," he added, still in Italian.

"Thank you," Deborah said gravely, a dimple appearing at the side of her mouth.

"Ah, you speak my language? How nice." He spoke in English now, still laughing. "You didn't tell me that, Matthew."

"I was unaware of it," Matthew said drily, looking at Deborah with slightly narrowed eyes. "She didn't tell me."

"I only know a few words," Deborah confessed.

"You only need a few," Signor Scalatio murmured with amusement.

"One usually seems enough," Deborah agreed.

He lifted his eyebrows in enquiry, his eyes on her.

"No," said Deborah, still grave. "I know that in about fifteen languages."

"A well-travelled young lady, and one who knows how to look after herself, obviously." He slid his eyes sideways to Matthew. "I admire your taste more than ever, my friend." That was back in Italian and again Deborah had to guess by context and might be wrong, but from the way they both laughed she suspected she was right. She carefully betrayed no sign of having understood that one, though.

"Is your stay in Venice to be a long one?" he asked Deborah, turning back to her.

"I'm afraid I'm only here for a week."

"A pity," said Signor Scalatio, sighing. "There is far too much of Venice for a week to be long enough."

"She has been here before," Matthew told him, "and likes it."

"But of course she does," Signor Scalatio said vigorously. "How could she not?" and gave Deborah another warm, admiring smile.

"Let me get you both a drink. What will you have, Deborah?" He had not asked her last name, accepting her without question as a friend of Matthew's, and she wondered if she would ever discover Matthew's last name. Judging from the clothes and moneyed air of the other guests she imagined she hadn't been wrong in guessing that Matthew was someone newsworthy. Catching sight of a woman on the far side of the room, she was certain of it because her, at least, Deborah recognised. But then most people who read a newspaper would recognise her. She was American by origin, a jetsetter by occupation and a lady with three husbands and a lot of alimony to her credit. Her presence at this party gave it a certain stamp; she wouldn't go anywhere unless it was the right sort of party.

Sipping the glass Signor Scalatio had handed her, Deborah carefully ran her eye over the other guests and was sure she had seen some of them before although she couldn't put a name to more than one or two.

They were circulating at the right sort of pace, moving from group to group with bright, fixed smiles. Diamonds flashed round slim necks, clean-shaven, predatory men smiled, voices rose and fell. Deborah thought yearningly of her nice, quiet hotel room, but still, you never knew. She might be on to something with Matthew. On the other hand, she thought grimly, she might not, and that would be both a waste of time and a bore.

These were the sort of people she would go a long way to avoid in ordinary circumstances. Making conversation with them was like pushing a snowball uphill in June.

"You haven't forgotten you're with me?" Matthew asked at her ear, his shoulder touching her own.

"How could I?" Deborah asked, eyeing him over the rim of her glass.

"You looked as if you weren't sure what you were doing here."

"I'm not sure," she agreed. "I must have been crazy to let you talk me into it."

"One good deed deserves another."

He stood facing her now, very close, looking down into her eyes and at this distance she could feel the sexual magnetism which made him so self-confident. You either had it or you hadn't, she thought with angry cynicism, and this man had and knew it. The very way he stood there, smiling so easily, relaxed down to his toes, told you that he had it made.

Signor Scalatio had been absorbed by some of the other guests and Matthew and Deborah were alone for a moment, but the brief instant when they stared into each other's eyes and Deborah prickled with irritation at his calm assurance was over very quickly. Several other guests joined them, greeting Matthew. He introduced her, but she did not catch their names. Their smiles were, in any case, perfunctory. It was Matthew they were interested in and they barely looked at her.

"The market's in a nervous state," one of them said in a lowered tone, as though discussing something dangerous.

Matthew shrugged. "When isn't it?"

"Another run on the fixed currencies?"

"You tell me," Matthew smiled, and his smile was intended to shut off that conversation, and did. The man fell silent, staring at his drink.

The woman beside him began to talk about the latest kidnapping. It was an Italian trade, almost a way of life. "I think I'll go back to Paris," she said nervously, and one got the feeling she was always in flight from something, never settled anywhere. "Things are quieter over there." She had ruby earrings dangling beside her face which swung in a little circle every time she moved her head. Worth a fortune, Deborah decided, watching them. No doubt she would be worth kidnapping for those alone.

"How long are you over here, Matthew?" the man asked. Everyone used Matthew's first name. It was maddening. She kept flicking over her cards in her computer-like brain, trying to track him down, always aware of that strong intuition that she ought to recognise him, by name if not by face. Over the years she had filed away hundreds of names and faces. People always tended to surface again somewhere, and a good memory was a blessing.

Another man wandered up and Deborah stiffened as she recognised him. He was an Italian of very good family who had been at the Italian legation in a Middle Eastern country some years back, and Deborah had met him at an official briefing. He hadn't said anything. He had been a junior diplomat. Throughout the briefing he had mainly been occupied with Deborah's blonde hair and long, slim legs.

He was occupied with them now. She could see that he couldn't quite place her but sensed they had met before. He edged closer, giving her a confiding smile.

"Haven't we met before?"

She caught the turn of Matthew's head, the faint, cynical smile. She smiled at the Italian. "I'm sure I'd remember if we had."

He liked that and despite his diplomatic training missed the evasion in it.

"Perhaps I've seen you in a newspaper or on TV," he suggested, obviously not sure whether she was a well-known face or not and not wishing her to realise that he didn't know.

"Perhaps you have," she returned lightly, telling him nothing.

"A beautiful dress," he murmured, falling back on a compliment in smiling resignation. "Such an interesting material." It gave him an excuse to finger the tiny capped sleeve nearest him, rubbing the edge of it between finger and thumb before tentatively brushing his hand along her naked arm.

Deborah watched him calmly. "I'm glad you like it. It's Italian, a man-made textile." It had all the smooth feel and delicate colour of real silk. She had chosen it because it would look equally at home at a formal reception or a private party. When she was on a story abroad she never knew what sort of invitations she would get, so her wardrobe had to be elastic and fit all occasions.

"How long are you staying in Venice?"

"A week." He had not taken his hand away. She hadn't protested, so now he was sliding a finger up and down her inner arm and moving closer, smiling confidently.

Deborah did not want to choke him off too abruptly; it might trigger his memory. He had sidled up to her after that briefing and tried this sort of approach and she had politely told him to get lost. A repeat performance might make his memory start working.

It was ironic, really, that after years of fending men off without a second thought she had fallen hook, line and sinker for someone like Robert. A friend of hers had once told her that she had a theory about love. "It doesn't exist. We invent it for ourselves, at a time and place of our own choosing. One day we just feel like being in love and choose the first object we see." Deborah had laughed, but she had been half convinced.

Her experience with Robert had confirmed in her the hostile cynicism about men which years of journalism had instilled in her. Working with them abroad, when they were away from their wives and bored, at a loose end in the evenings, looking for some amusement, she had often had passes from colleagues. It had become second nature to see them coming and either duck or coolly rebuff them. The unmarried ones were more persistent. They imagined that because she was free too that meant she was available. Refusals got them on the raw and they became sulky and difficult to work with, which was tiresome.

Deborah was ambitious and intelligent. From an early age she had had her eyes set on climbing in her career. Not many women went in for foreign news. They didn't like the travelling or the danger they could run into—they preferred to stay safely at home. You had to be a special breed to go in for foreign reporting. "You have to be as tough as leather," Hal had told her some years back. "Are you that tough?"

"Yes," she had said as coolly as though she believed it, but, of course, her confidence had largely been pretence.

She had found that if you act as though you know what you're doing, people believe it. Confidence was everything. People accept you at your own valuation unless you prove them wrong.

The Italian was talking softly, gazing into her eyes. He thought he was getting somewhere with her and Deborah wondered how she was going to shed him without trouble.

She needn't have worried. Matthew moved in quietly, sliding an arm around her waist. "Enjoying yourself, darling?"

She hid her surprise with some difficulty. Smiling, she nodded. "It's a lovely party."

"I'm glad you think so." His blue eyes glanced down sideways at her. Despite his smile, they had a sort of hardness which they hadn't had before.

The other man looked from one to the other of them in comprehending resignation, murmured something polite and vanished.

"You're full of surprises," Matthew told her.

"Oh?"

"I hadn't got you down as a flirt."

"What had you got me down as?"

"I'm not sure, but not that."

"I see—you work on the principle of elimination, do you?"

He laughed, eyeing her speculatively. "With you I can see I'm going to have to."

"Cryptic but interesting," Deborah agreed.

"Do you like Modigliani?"

The question made her laugh. "Isn't he the man who painted with one eye shut?"

Matthew ignored that. "There's one of his sketches somewhere around. Scalatio's very proud of it. It cost a fortune and is now worth twice as much."

"That's one criterion," Deborah nodded.

"Like to see it?"

"Very much. I like those long, slightly askew ladies of his."

"It's all a question of how you see things."

"Very true."

Matthew's lips twitched. "What a demure little cat you can sound—but don't think I can't see the claws."

He ushered her down the enormous room and she felt people glancing at them with polite curiosity. It annoyed her to admit to herself that Matthew grew on you. He had more intelligence than that long-limbed athlete's physique suggested and she was sorry they hadn't met before she ran into Robert. She could have liked him a good deal if she hadn't been seeing him through a distorting mirror. Every time she had a second of inactivity Robert came shooting into her mind, destroying her peace. Pain was unbearably constant, like a faithful dog one could not shoo away.

The Modigliani was hanging in a white-walled little room off the grand *sala*. There were several other pictures displayed next to it, but it had an insistence which kept one looking at it rather than the others.

The harsh, swift black lines of charcoal leapt out of the frame. Matthew was watching Deborah, rather than the sketch.

"Like it?"

"Yes," she said, turning her head to meet his eyes.

"You're so forthcoming you deafen me," Matthew said wryly.

"Do you want me to talk about the technical merits? I can't, I'm no art expert. I like it. What else can I say?" She moved to look at one of the other pictures and Matthew moved at the same moment. They skidded. His arm went round her and on a reflex impulse she pushed him away, although a second later she realised it had been a purely polite instinct on his part. Her little shove annoyed him, though, and he looked at her impatiently.

"Don't get your hackles up, I wasn't making a pass."

Flushing, she muttered something inaudible, annoyed with herself.

"Although it's an idea," he said, getting angrier. "I hate to disappoint a lady."

"Don't be stupid!" Deborah flared, taking another step backward. "I'm in no mood for that old routine."

"That's obvious, and it's just as obvious why, but I don't like getting handed off before I've even thought of doing anything."

It was at that point that she should have apologised, soothed him down, because his face was tight and angry and his blue eyes had a brightness which was due to rage, not excitement. Deborah briefly meant to, but at the last second she felt an impulse of sexual hostility and instead snapped: "Just keep your hands to yourself!"

It pushed him over the edge, as she might have expected. His lips drew in harshly, his hands shot out to grab her. The sexual hostility wasn't all on her side now. The instinct to hit back was uppermost in Matthew, his jawline aggressive.

"I don't like paying bills for other people," he bit out as he began to pull her towards him.

Deborah's shoulders were clamped by hard, clenched fingers, so she kicked him viciously on the shins, struggling against the pressure drawing her closer to him.

"Ouch!" he grunted, shifting back but not relinquishing his hold on her. "That hurt!" He rubbed one leg on the other, the blue eyes furious. "My God, you almost broke my leg!"

"Let me go or I'll do it next time!" she snapped.

"You won't get the chance, you little bitch!" The force propelling her forwards intensified. She was slammed into him, held, while he bent his head to kiss her. Deborah twisted her face away, wriggling, his thigh pushed against hers. He released her shoulders to put his arms round her to hold her and she took the opportunity to duck down and out of his grasp. Matthew swore under his breath and reached for her again. His hand caught the back of her dress so roughly that the thin silken material tore. Matthew was startled into pulling his arm back, but he forgot to let go of her dress. The silk went with him, splitting with a noise which seemed deafening in the silence.

Deborah swivelled and the tear ran right across the dress so that it hung free of her body.

They both froze in a stunned tableau, neither able to say a word. At that moment the door behind them opened and in walked Teresa Scalatio with the bright, fixed smile of someone who is about to make an excuse for appearing at all. The smile was wiped away as she took in Deborah's torn dress, the looks on their faces.

The flood of Italian came with a hiss like fifty vipers and for once Matthew seemed incapable of stemming it. He was standing there, his hands hanging at his sides, looking like someone who has been poleaxed.

When he did break out of his horror he moved quickly, striding across the room to thrust Teresa out of the door again, talking back in her tongue.

Deborah held the tear in her dress together and wondered how the hell she was going to get out of the apartment without the most appalling embarrassment.

Matthew came back and closed the door, leaning against it, looking at her with glacial fixity.

"I'm not going to apologise. You brought that on yourself."

"I know," she admitted wearily. "I lost my temper."

He drew in his lower lip between his teeth, let it go with a faint impatient sigh. "So did I—and I do apologise. It was a bloody ridiculous way to behave. I'm not in the habit of tearing women's clothes off. Not in public, anyway." That last sentence was added with a wry little grin, self-mocking.

"What you do in private is your own affair." Even as she came back with that Deborah was regretting the impulse to humour which was out of place.

He laughed, though, and it relaxed the tension between them and suddenly it all seemed so funny that both of them began to laugh at the same moment.

"That poor girl's face," Deborah muttered, leaning against the smooth white wall and shaking with amusement and a sort of compassion. "God knows what she thought we'd been up to!"

"I know too," Matthew confessed. "She was very explicit. The young of today have a forthright turn of phrase, don't you find? When I was sixteen I would never have dreamt of saying some of things she just said to me."

"Sixteen?" Deborah checked her laughter. "She looks older."

"She's quite precocious," Matthew shrugged.

"So it seems. And with mature tastes, too."

He made a little face. "Me, you mean? Oh, she'll

grow out of her crush on me, but at the moment it's very awkward.''

"I can imagine.''

"I don't want to hurt her feelings more than I can help, but I'm not in the habit of seducing little girls, however precocious.''

"Appearances can be deceptive,'' Deborah murmured.

"Meaning what?'' He stared at her, his face stiffening again.

"You say you aren't in the habit of tearing women's clothes off, but Teresa could be excused for believing otherwise after tonight.''

"My God, you're right,'' he groaned. "I'm too quick-tempered.''

"You had provocation.'' Deborah looked down at her dress. "How am I going to get out of here like this?''

"Don't worry, I'll find you a coat.'' He opened the door, looked back at her with a mischievous face. "You're a very belligerent lady. I feel I was lucky to get off with a kicked shin!''

He had gone before she could retort and she laughed silently as the door shut behind him. Looking down ruefully at her dress, she thought that she should have asked if he could find some safety pins. The dress was beyond repair, of course. Who would have thought that that material would have torn so easily? It had ripped at amazing speed on a diagonal, rather like a run appearing in a pair of hose. She held it together experimentally and caught the sardonic dark eyes of the girl in the Modigliani who had watched the whole scene with that odd, archaic smile.

"It's all right for you," Deborah told her, moving to where she could stare back. The great almond-shaped eyes held a depth of ironic amusement. "You're safe enough in there—they can't get at you."

If you tampered with a man's ego you never knew what sort of monsters you were unleashing. Pride was a fetish with them. They reacted violently to any sort of implied slight. If she had been chasing Matthew, no doubt he would have run like mad, but since she seemed indifferent he had become angry in a flash.

She had half doubted his story about Teresa until she saw the girl's glowing, eager face as she flung herself at him. Teresa was drowning in the sort of passion which in adolescence can be traumatic. Her eyes ate Matthew every time they looked at him. Matthew was in flight from the poor child, which was admirable, because Teresa might only be sixteen, but she looked older and she was a very attractive little creature, perhaps more beautiful than she would be ever again in her life. She had the radiant inner glow of love to light her face and that dewy youth to go with it. Matthew might well have been tempted. Some men would have been. Maybe he had been tempted; something must have lit the torch Teresa was carrying. But now he was running, for all the implied flattery to his ego.

The door opened again and he was back. Over his arm he carried a coat which made Deborah gasp. It was a full-length white mink. She didn't even dare hazard a guess at the price.

"My God!" she exclaimed.

"Like it?" He grinned at her. "Will it fit, though?" He held it for her chivalrously and she slid her arms into the sleeves. Matthew stood back and regarded her, head to one side.

"Nice," he said. "Mink is definitely your fur."

Deborah smoothed the white pelts, snuggling into it. "I've always wondered what it would feel like."

"To wear mink? You mean none of your admirers offered to give you one? How remiss! I'm glad to remedy their omission."

"Whose is it?" She looked up. "Not Teresa's?"

His face was wry. "Don't take it off."

"How did you persuade her to lend it to me?"

"I didn't," he said. "I asked her father, and he told her."

"Oh, dear! Do you think that was wise?"

"We've got to get you out of here without causing a lot of nasty talk. I don't want to find myself in the Italian papers tomorrow. This is just the sort of anecdote they love."

In all the excitement Deborah hadn't looked at it from that angle. She almost laughed aloud. She had been half hoping to pick up some good news story, but she hadn't hoped to be part of it herself. That was just what it was, though—a high society party, some rich and not unknown guests, and a scandal involving one of them ripping the clothes off another. I could sell it to one of the Rome scandal sheets for a very tidy sum, Deborah thought. Pity I don't fancy reading my own name in one of them. It would pay for my holiday.

"I'm afraid Teresa is going to hate you after tonight," she told Matthew.

"My shoulders are broad enough to bear that. Her

father seemed rather relieved. I think he was a bit worried about it all.''

"Did he fear your intentions?" Deborah grinned at him mockingly.

"He didn't say, but I fancy he did." Matthew looked wry, the blue eyes holding hers. "My reputation, alas."

"Oh, have you got one?"

"As reluctant as I am to admit it, yes."

She could believe it. The experienced, cynical smile reinforced her suspicions about him. Who was he? she thought again. I'd swear I've seen him somewhere. There was a lot more to him than she had thought at first. He had humour, charm, enough energy for three men, a great deal of self-control and a temper which overrode it at times. An interesting combination. His physical attraction she found easy to resist. She had to admit she found it harder to ignore the amused little smile, the wry blue eyes. She did not want to like him, she wasn't liking men much at all at present, but she did, annoying though she found it.

Matthew stepped closer and adjusted her collar, lifting it so that it framed her face. "Charming." He smiled down into her eyes. "They'll never notice anything odd. Just saunter through the room without a care in the world."

"I feel like that model girl I'm not," Deborah confided as she followed him. "Mink is definitely my style."

Matthew gave her a funny glinting smile. "Is that a hint?"

She went through the door he was holding open. "Sorry, no."

"*You're* sorry," he said, mocking her. "I've got a

feeling mink would be a small price to pay.''

"How flattering!" Everyone was turning to look at them and she had a sudden, sinking suspicion that they all knew exactly what had happened in the little room. She pinned a casual smile on her face and strolled along beside Matthew, all the same, pretending not to notice the stares, the whispers, the curious amused smiles.

Teresa didn't come near them. She stood next to a trailing green fern, turning a glass in her hand, her face very flushed and a brittle smile twisting her cherry pink mouth. Deborah hoped whe was imagining the spite in that smile, but she didn't think she was.

Teresa's sloe-like eyes examined the mink coat with a sort of caged ferocity. She didn't look surprised to see Deborah wearing it, but she certainly didn't look pleased. It was rather shorter than it should have been, of course, as Deborah was taller. She was slender, though, and the coat wrapped round her rather elegantly, she felt. Yes, definitely, she told herself as she caught a reflection of herself as they passed a mirror, mink was her style. Pity she couldn't afford one of her own.

What was a girl of sixteen doing with a coat like this, anyway? Matthew had said she was spoilt, and obviously he hadn't underestimated it. A father who bought mink coats for a kid of that age needed his head tested. And had money to burn.

Emerging into the cool radiance of the Venetian moonlight, she paused to sigh with relief. So far, so good.

"Feel better?" Matthew enquired.

"Much," she admitted.

They walked along towards the steps. The gondola

was waiting for them, but as they began to descend, carefully negotiating the slippery wet stone, another gondola skimmed into view and a thin young man leapt from it with an acrobatic agility which so surprised Deborah that she halted to stare at him in open-mouthed admiration.

That was before she noticed his camera.

"Oh, hell!" Matthew muttered, but he was behind her and on the narrow steps it was impossible for him to get past to save the situation.

The young man moved so fast Deborah had the dazed feeling of someone in an accident. His hand flicked out and she had no time to grab at the mink coat as he flung it apart. She had been using her hands to stabilise herself as she went down the tricky steps. The flash blub dazzled her. A look of comical horror on her face, she dragged the coat together, spluttering wordlessly, but the unbalanced movement made her slip on the mossy stone. Matthew dived to catch her as she toppled sideways, giving a wild shriek. The flashbulbs exploded around them like lightning.

Matthew's language was almost as colourful. Breaking off the outbreak of angry words, he pushed Deborah to the wall unceremoniously, growled: "Stay there," and flung himself down the steps.

He was too late by a whisker. Seeing him coming, the boy leapt back into the gondola with the same agility and speed with which he had landed. It smoothly steered away. Matthew came to a halt on the lowest step, clearly hesitating about whether to follow or not, and the boy called back cheerfully: "*Ciao, grazie*, Signor Tyrell!"

Tyrell, Matthew Tyrell. The name went crash inside

Deborah's head like brass cymbals and with it came a host of remembered clippings from the morgue. Matthew Tyrell was the head of an international drug firm. She had researched him and his company four years ago. *Probe* had done a series of articles on them. A drug they had been manufacturing had proved to have unfortunate side effects; they hadn't tested it sufficiently, rushing it on the market far too early. Deborah couldn't imagine how she had forgotten his face—but then she had been more interested in the story than the man behind it. Most of her work on the story had been done researching in the morgue, the library of past stories which could be so helpful to a reporter. She remembered that Matthew Tyrell had had a bulging file behind his name.

Oh, he was newsworthy, all right. He was just up the *paparazzi*'s street. My God, thought Deborah, suddenly realising that he wasn't the only one involved, what have I got myself into? A picture of her in a torn dress, lurching back into Matthew's arms, was going to be splashed all over the Italian press tomorrow.

CHAPTER FOUR

AS SHE WAS GETTING INTO BED later that night, Deborah's eye caught the mink coat which she had carefully hung just inside her wardrobe, and she looked at it appreciatively. She could get used to wearing coats like that very easily. About to put out the light, she had a horrifying vision of someone breaking into the room and making off with the mink. How much was it worth? Thousands, she thought. She was in sole custody of a small fortune. She suddenly felt very worried.

It had not occurred to her until now, but while the coat was in her possession she was presumably responsible for it. It would take her years to pay for a coat like that and if it was stolen she would have to pay the Scalatio family whatever it was worth.

It must be insured, she told herself. Of course it must. She put out the light and settled to sleep, but sleep refused to come. She listened to the night sounds beyond the window, prickling with anxiety.

After a quarter of an hour she crossly switched on the light again and got out of bed. Shrugging into her dressing-gown, she collected the mink. He could afford to take the risk of losing it. She couldn't.

They had parted on the stairs. Deborah had the impression Matthew Tyrell had been intending to make some effort to stop whatever news coverage might be about to break. He had been grimly absorbed in private thoughts all the way back to the hotel. Deborah had not tried to interrupt them; she had worries of her own.

She wouldn't have found it easy to get to sleep anyway with the prospect of becoming a very public part of Matthew Tyrell's very public life hanging over her, but the coat was just too much. He could have it in his room for the night.

It was several moments before he opened the door, and when he did he stared blankly at her.

"Can you look after this for tonight? I can't sleep with it in my room—I'm scared stiff a thief will break in and steal it."

He ran one hand through his already tousled hair, impatience in every line of his lean body. "God almighty, what irrelevant minds women have!"

"There's nothing irrelevant about having a coat worth thousands of pounds in my room. I couldn't afford to replace it if it got stolen."

"It wouldn't be your responsiblity."

"I'm not going to take the risk."

"Oh, give it here," he muttered, snatching at it.

They heard heavy breathing behind them, someone wheezing as they climbed the stairs. Deborah caught the shuffle of feet, saw a man's head coming up through the open stairway.

Matthew Tyrell shot a look past her, growled under his breath and the next moment had pulled her through the door and shut it.

"We can't afford any more trouble," he said, bending his head to listen as the footsteps shuffled past.

Deborah glanced at the room. He had not been to bed yet. The white telephone sat on the bed beside a telephone directory. She had the distinct idea he had been making a series of calls in his effort to stop anyone printing that picture.

Matthew flung the mink across a chair and Deborah winced. "Don't treat it like that! Have you no soul?"

"Very little," he said. His dark blue eyes had an air of strain, she noticed. The lines round them were intensified. "I'm trying to find a way of keeping you out of the limelight, but of course the more I try to protect you the more curious the vultures will get."

"How chivalrous of you to try to protect me!" Somehow she couldn't keep a note of sarcasm out of her voice, and Matthew picked it up, giving her a direct, cool stare.

"I'm used to it. You're not. It can be unpleasant."

She wasn't quite sure that it was her welfare he was really worried about, but she gave him the benefit of the doubt and smiled at him.

"It's very kind of you to be so concerned."

She shouldn't have used such formal language. He misunderstood it and his brows jerked together.

"Very well, don't believe me." He turned away, tightening the belt of his short robe. Deborah realised what she hadn't noticed before. He was not wearing a thing under it. His long legs were bare, the dark hair on them faintly damp. He had been taking a shower when she rapped at his door.

The realisation made her nervous. She edged towards the door and he turned and caught the movement, his frown deepening.

"Now what's the matter?" he demanded.

"I'd better slip out while the coast is clear," said Deborah, not quite meeting his eyes.

He came back towards her and she shifted backwards involuntarily. Matthew stopped dead, his eyes fixed on her.

"I'm not about to pounce again," he bit out.

"I didn't think you were!" But she had flushed and she still couldn't meet his eyes.

"Oh, yes, you did. Don't jump like that, it makes me lose my temper."

"We wouldn't want that," Deborah flashed furiously, looking up at him now. "Last time was bad enough!"

"Don't you learn from experience?"

"No," she said, remembering Robert. "Apparently not."

"Time you started, then."

Their voices had risen without their noticing and suddenly they did realise it and both of them fell silent, looking at each other.

"I get the feeling I've been here before," Matthew groaned, giving her a wry little grin.

"*Déjà vu*," she agreed with equal dryness. "I'm sorry."

"If you can just get it fixed in your mind that I'm not intent on raping you we might steer clear of these nasty little moments."

Deborah laughed, flushing. "Right. Got it."

"Good," he said with amusement and a more relaxed expression. "Now I'm going to come past you to peer outside and check that there are no *paparazzi* lurking about, so please don't start flying into a panic when I come within a foot of you."

"I'm not a complete fool," she protested, smiling.

"No, just a woman."

"Chauvinist!"

He opened the door and peered out. "Seems okay," he said, turning towards her.

Deborah sighed with relief. The intimacy of their situation, with Matthew half-naked and herself in her nightie and dressing-gown, had begun to make her nerves prickle. Sliding past him, she whispered, "Goodnight again, then."

He laughed under his breath. There was that glint of mischief in his eyes again, but she only saw it for a second before he had bent towards her, saying softly, "I really think I must," and brushed his mouth against her own.

Just behind them was the glass door of the dumb waiter. It was suddenly pushed upwards. A flashbulb went off and Matthew in a split second of realisation had pushed Deborah away and was racing towards it.

Over his shoulders she saw the disappearing head and recognised the thin young man who had caught them on the steps outside the palazzo.

Matthew peered down the dumb waiter, then turned and raced for the stairs, his bare feet padding on the stone. Deborah put her hands over her face.

I don't believe it, she thought. How could he be so stupid? But then she realised that with or without that kiss the young man would have got a shot of them together in that betraying intimacy. The kiss merely underlined what their night attire would have suggested.

She went back into Matthew's room and sat down on the bed, staring at her fur slippers, jiggling them up and down like a child. She was past swearing or feeling angry. She just waited for him to come back.

When he did she could tell from his grim expression that he hadn't caught the young man.

"He was off in a flash," he said, shutting the door. "Why the hell couldn't you stay in your own room? What a stupid risk to take, coming down here like that!" Then he stopped, staring at her, his blue eyes narrowing and hardening. "Well, well, well," he drawled slowly after a moment's pause. "That hadn't occurred to me."

Deborah gazed patiently at him. "What hadn't?" she prompted when he didn't say anything more.

"Stupid of me," he said. "I should have thought of it before, but I was a bit slow on the uptake for once."

"What are you talking about now? Could I have a tiny clue?"

"Oh, yes, I think so," he said in an oddly ominous smooth tone, coming over to her.

She should have realised earlier, but she had reached a sort of indifferent calm after the catastrophes of the night and she had stopped flinching every time he came near her.

"I don't like being set up," said Matthew as he lifted her from the bed in a swift, angry movement.

"Hey—" Deborah began furiously.

She didn't have a chance to say anything else for a while. Matthew held her like a doll between his gripping hands, and in her stupefaction at his abrupt change of mood, Deborah was taken off guard. His mouth was forced down against her own, bruising it open. When she struggled and made muffled, furious noises, he took one hand from her shoulders and grasped her throat, pushing her head back so that she was unable to escape.

The fierceness of the kiss hurt. Her lips began to burn and then to go numb. She had her eyes wide open. Her hands pummelled at his chest, but they had no effect whatever. He was imposing all his superior male strength without mercy.

As she twisted in his grip her legs met the end of the bed. She felt herself falling and tried to save herself by gripping his shirt, but all that did was to bring Matthew with her.

The weight of his hard body crushed all the air out of her lungs for a moment. Matthew paused for a few seconds, his mouth lifted, a hard glinting brightness in the blue eyes as they stared down at her.

"We're where you intended all along, are we?" he asked in a voice she didn't like at all. "I must say you're nothing if not inventive. I've met some shrewd operators in my time, but you're something else. You had me fooled from the minute we met in that mist. The lost, sad stuff was brilliant. What are you? An actress?"

"Will you get off me?" Deborah burst out roughly, pushing at him.

"That's not what you want at all, is it?" His smile was no smile at all. His eyes were like cold little blue stones. "Was it your own idea? Or is the camera artist your boy-friend?"

"Look—" she began.

"No," he said harshly, "you look. Okay, I'll buy. Don't let's beat around the bush. I recognise the pitch now. It isn't the first time I've met black-mailers.''

"My God!" Deborah burst out again.

"Shut up," he muttered with a fury which leapt out at her from the blue eyes. He kissed her again, grinding her lip back on her teeth. When he lifted his head again she almost expected to see her own blood on his mouth. She probed the inner skin of her lip with her tongue, her eyes hating him.

"I'll pay up meekly—but first I want a little more value for my money."

There was no mistaking the tenor of that, even if his eyes hadn't underlined it with a swift, stripping glance over her.

"Oh, no, you don't," Deborah said fiercely.

"That's where you're wrong, lady, because I do." One of his hands fell against her breast and she stiffened in a sudden icy panic. She couldn't look away from his face. He might be violently angry, but there was something else in the blue eyes, and it made her face burn with colour. She saw his mouth twist.

"You *are* an actress," he mocked. "A clever one, too. You even blush to order. I've heard of actresses who can cry on cue, but that's something new to me. You really are surprising!"

While he was talking in that hostile, distasteful voice his long fingers were moving. Heat ran under Deborah's skin wherever they touched. Her body was reacting in a way she could not disguise. Matthew caressed her breast, watching her, and her heart began knocking fast against her breastbone.

The dryness of her mouth had silenced her for a moment. Matthew Tyrell gave another of his sharp, angry smiles.

"That's better. I suppose a straight approach hadn't occurred to you? You underestimate yourself, Deborah. Is that really your name? It doesn't matter—I like it. It suits you, as Scalatio said. It would have saved you and your boy-friend a lot of time and trouble if you'd cut out all the cloak and dagger stuff and just made me a direct offer."

His hand had slid down the flat plane of her stomach and she gave a little gasp as it touched her thigh. He gave her a little glance. "I fancied you the minute I saw you. You wouldn't have found me ungenerous. I don't generally go in for one-night stands, of course, but we could have discussed it in a rather more friendly fashion than this and I've no doubt we could have come to an arrangement."

Deborah's shocked panic had worn off now. She was lying very still, listening to the insults, her mind working overtime. She could see that no way was she going to convince him at the moment. That temper of his had the upper hand. Although he was no longer violent he was very angry, and on top of that he was getting sexually excited—she knew enough about men to recognise the way he was looking at her, the way he was touching her. For all his rage at what he thought she had done he was an opportunist, like all men. He was taking advantage of what he imagined the situation was, and he wasn't going to be convinced by any protests on her part.

The male animal was uppermost in him at this moment. She had felt a brief flicker of excitement herself when he was touching her breasts, but it was an involuntary physical reaction which was partly born out of anger. The adrenalin was running high in both of them. The atmosphere had become explosive with tension. She had to do something to lessen it, but her mind wasn't working too clearly.

She shifted under him, saying: "There's something digging into my shoulder blades."

Whatever he had expected her to say it hadn't been that, and his eyes flickered.

"Would you move for a moment, please?" Deborah didn't make the mistake of sounding sharp. She gave him a little smile, her eyes wide and innocent.

She saw him hesitate, then he shrugged and the weight of his body lifted. Deborah sat up, and they both looked at the bed. A book lay on it. Matthew reached over and picked it up, tossed it to the floor.

"I realise you're not going to believe this, but you're wrong," said Deborah, not bothering to try to run. He would catch her before she got to the door. Deborah was a girl who faced facts. She sat there and looked at him quite calmly, and he stared back, his face unreadable.

"I've got as much reason as you have for not wanting to become part of a jet-set scandal. You haven't been set up by me." She could see that his temper was cooling slightly. She had distracted him with her complaint about the book. She was beginning to know Matthew Tyrell. His temper shot up quickly but it cooled quickly too. All she had to do was keep him listening until it was right down to normal.

"Do you really expect me to believe that?"

"Not at the moment," she admitted, shrugging. "I

could give you my word of honour, but as you don't believe I've got one I don't suppose that would do any good. I can prove that I have a perfectly respectable background in London, but at this time of night it wouldn't be easy for you to check—and anyway, I resent the implication that I need to do that.''

Her even tone was having an effect, although he was still watching her with very cold eyes.

''I've been thinking about the opportune appearance of that cameraman,'' she went on slowly. ''If I didn't tip him off, I think I can guess who did and why.''

Matthew Tyrell stiffened, pushing one hand into the pocket of his black robe. That dragged down the lapel and Deborah saw the smooth skin of his shoulder briefly before she looked away.

The last thing she needed at this moment was any awareness of him as a man. She had to keep the temperature as cool as she could.

''Well?'' he demanded.

''Your little friend Teresa, I suspect,'' said Deborah. The thought had been nagging away at her for some time, but she had told herself that if the girl had tipped off the *paparazzi* she had done it in the heat of the moment. Jealousy was an ungovernable emotion. Deborah hadn't wanted to make Matthew Tyrell angry with the girl. Self-preservation was more important at this moment, though. If it came to a choice between herself and Teresa Scalatio she had no choice at all. She wasn't getting raped in anger by Matthew Tyrell.

He swung away, the movement terse and abrupt. She waited, watching the long spine, the tousled dark hair. She saw his hand clench inside his pocket.

"That hadn't occurred to me," he said, and now he was thinking very hard.

"It should have done. How was I to know you were going to rip my dress off at that party? How could I have a cameraman waiting outside to snap something I didn't know was going to happen?"

He muttered something explosive under his breath.

"Not very logical of you," Deborah murmured.

"Don't be so bloody patronising!" He turned, giving her a direct, hard stare. "How do I know this isn't a double bluff?"

Deborah gave him an unworried smile. "You don't know. If I was the sort of creature you think I am, I wouldn't be worried about going to bed with you. I'd probably be leaping in like a greyhound."

His mouth twitched. "What an interesting picture!"

"You can forget it," Deborah informed him. "I'm neither a blackmailer nor a wicked lady. I don't want to go to bed with you, and I certainly don't want those pictures of us in the papers."

He sat down on the bed beside her and ran both hands through his hair until it stood on end like the quills of a porcupine. "Hell, this is the second time tonight I've had to apologise to you. It's getting to be a habit."

"You did warn me you had a nasty temper."

"Not nasty," he protested. "Just hot."

Deborah made no comment about that and he laughed softly. "It makes sense," he muttered. "Italians go in for revenge in a big way—all that opera they got shovelled down their throats at an early age, I suppose. This is just the sort of trick Teresa would pull. I told you she was dangerous. I shudder to think what she'll be like when she's thirty. At sixteen she's a menace.''

"She's in love," Deborah said tolerantly, so relieved that he had become human again that she smiled.

"You're very understanding. I can't say I'd feel so indulgent towards her in your shoes." Matthew swivelled his head to look at the phone. "I don't feel very indulgent, myself. I've a good mind to ring her father and kick up a song and dance about it.''

"Not without proof," Deborah said mildly. "You do tend to jump in at the deep end without checking if there's any water, don't you?"

He looked amused. "No, not normally. You have a disastrous effect on me."

"How typical of a man to blame a woman!"

"We can't help it, it's the original sin," said Matthew, laughing.

"Who wrote the Bible? Not a woman," Deborah said drily.

"You're a very exceptional woman," said Matthew, his eyes on her. "I don't think I've met one quite like you before. I've only known you for twenty-four hours, but you leave me speechless."

"Now *that* I hadn't noticed!"

"You have an almost masculine mind," he said, laughing.

"If you imagine that is a compliment, think again."

His laughter deepened and he reached out a hand carefully to touch her cheek, his fingers gentle. "Did I apologise?"

"I think you did."

"Adequately?" He was moving closer and Deborah sensed another shift in his feelings.

"Perfectly," she said, getting up. She didn't want him starting again.

"He must be crazy," said Matthew, rising too.

Deborah looked at him blankly.

"The man who walked out on you," Matthew expanded, watching her.

"Oh, him," said Deborah, her smile vanishing. She hadn't thought of Robert for what seemed years. It could only be a matter of half an hour or so, in fact, but her mind had been so totally occupied with the present that the past had lost its sting. Now it came back with all its attendant pain and humiliation. She walked to the door, keeping her face averted from Matthew Tyrell.

"Let me," he said, opening the door. She felt the quick penetrating look he gave her and fought to keep the pain out of her eyes. She didn't want observers, however sympathetic, to see it.

"We don't want to give the *paparazzi* a hat-trick," he said as he glanced up and down the stone-floored passage. "It looks okay."

"Goodnight, and let's hope this time I don't have to say it again," Deborah murmured, moving past him.

She didn't have any trouble reaching her room unobserved. The hotel was still and quiet. She slid out of her dressing gown and got into bed, yawning. My God, I'm tired, she thought, as she clicked off the light. Lying in the dark, she listened to the waters washing along the stone steps and lapping the sides of the *riva*.

There had been a dangerous moment when Matthew Tyrell was touching her and she had had a stupid, wild impulse to let him do what he wanted to do. It had seemed briefly to be what she wanted too. She had been in emotional turmoil ever since she realised Robert didn't feel the way she had thought he felt. Matthew's anger and desire had been echoed inside herself until her mind surfaced from its temporary haze and she began to think clearly.

He had an unpredictable temper, that man. It shot up like mercury and took one by surprise. It came down again, of course, and when he wasn't in a temper he was a man one could like very easily.

Except, she reminded herself, that men were on the taboo list for her at present.

She had already got more involved with Matthew Tyrell than she had ever imagined she would, and she had a horrible feeling that she hadn't seen the last of him, not by a long chalk. Tomorrow they might be caught in the eye of a little storm of publicity. I ought to ring Hal to warn him, she thought, then she yawned again. Plenty of time for that tomorrow. Her body ached and her mind was unable to hold thought for very long. She drifted off to sleep with the sound of the Venetian waters making a calming background noise.

She woke up to hammering on the door. Dazed, sleepy-eyed, she staggered out of the bed and picked up her dressing gown, taking in the morning light with a wince.

As she slipped into her dressing gown she opened the door. Matthew Tyrell flashed past, giving her a glimpse of dark rage and fierce blue eyes.

Deborah shut the door and leaned on it, a hand over her yawning mouth. "Not so early!" she wailed. "I'm barely awake."

"You lying little bitch!" he burst out, glaring.

"Not again," she said on a weary sigh.

"It's out of the bag," he grated through his teeth.

"What is?" She didn't move from the door. She needed the support of the heavy wooden panels behind her drooping shoulders. The cool Venetian light was like stabbing daggers on her retina.

"The cat, Miss Linton."

For a moment that didn't register. She glanced at the newspaper in his hand.

"Oh, yes," he said unpleasantly, "it's all here. So you aren't an actress or a model, you're a bloody journalist."

How did the *paparazzi* discover that? Deobrah wondered, and then her mind came up with the answer. They would have found out who she was from the hotel porter. Hotel porters are always talkative if the price is right. Her passport would have told them she was a journalist.

Foreign visitors always had to be registered. She should have thought of that last night.

"I knew you were up to something!" Matthew Tyrell raged, his hand clenching on the newspaper. He flung it across the room with a violent gesture. It lay at her feet and she looked down and got a shock as she saw the photograph splashed across the page.

"What a terrible picture of me!" she exclaimed.

Matthew Tyrell said something she preferred to ignore.

"Well, you're used to being in the papers," she said. "I'm not. Not one of my friends would recognise me from that. I look like a harpy!"

"You said it, not me."

"My head aches and I'm dead with lack of sleep,"

she sighed. "Don't shout like that! There's a man sitting on the back of my head banging on it with a hammer."

"I may join him," grated Matthew.

Deborah sighed. "I'm sorry, I admit I should have told you I was a journalist—but after you'd made your views of journalists plain I decided discretion was the better part of valour."

"Not to mention that you're a deceitful little bitch," he said viciously.

"Not to mention that," Deborah agreed.

There was a second when he almost laughed, but his temper had the better of him. He looked at her with a sort of bottled rage.

"And to think I apologised to you last night! I've always prided myself on being fairly good at character reading, but I've been way off beam with you."

"You still are," she said wearily.

"Oh, no, I think not. How much was in it for you?"

"Not a penny." She was beginning to get angry herself. "Look, what possible use do you think it is to me to have this sort of story about myself in the papers?"

"I can think of several uses you could make of it. Read the story."

Deborah bent and picked up the paper. Bending made her head thud and she moved away from the door, a hand to it, wincing.

Her own name leapt out of the print, but she was too dull this morning to be able to fight her way through the rest of the Italian sentences.

"What does it say?" she asked.

"Your Italian not up to it? Sure?" He wasn't going to

believe a syllable she uttered from now on, she could see that.

"Don't tell if if you don't want to—I really don't care," she shrugged.

"They politely describe you as my new friend," he drawled, "but I think we're both adult enough to know what they mean by that."

"Well, I didn't think they were going to suggest we were just good friends," Deborah pointed out. She had known just what sort of implication those pictures would carry with them and so had he. So why make all this fuss now?

"I'm sure you knew precisely what sort of angle they would suggest."

"Of course I knew—so did you. What's your point?"

"My point?" Matthew took a long stride, his lips drawn back over his teeth in a sort of snarl. "You were in at the planning stage, weren't you? It was all a carefully worked out trap."

"Oh, don't be stupid! Do you think anyone would go to all that trouble just to get that rubbish into a paper?"

"Reporters will sell their grandmothers for a story."

"I'm not that sort of reporter." Why had she ever thought he was an intelligent man? He was fixated on this belief that people were always trying to trap him.

"What sort are you, then?" he asked, quick as a whip, and she saw then that her next answer was not going to make her any more popular with him.

She hesitated. "I'm with the *Probe* team," she said.

For a split second he did not move. A variety of expressions chased across his face, and Deborah didn't like any of them. "My God," he said on a long breath. "My God, it's worse than I'd thought!"

"Of course, it would be," Deborah muttered under her breath. No, he wasn't a very intelligent man. She could see that he was about to explode again and this time it was going to be quite an explosion. His eyes were flashing like warning signals.

"That's the collection of vermin who tried a character assassination on me when we had a little trouble with a new drug."

"Several people died, as I recall it," Deborah flung back. "The drug hadn't been fully tested, or tested for long enough."

"There was an unexpected side effect which we couldn't have foreseen."

"It would have shown up if you'd kept up your tests for a few more years."

"And in those years a lot of people might have lived much more painful lives. That drug was a major break-through. You didn't bother to make that point, as I recall it." He paused in the harsh, angry outburst. "You were on the story, I take it?"

"Yes," she admitted.

"I see." He saw a lot more than that and he was dead wrong, but this time he wasn't going to listen to a word she said. His face was taut and a dark, angry red. The blue eyes were glacial.

"I must say you have a long memory on *Probe.* Why wait so long? Why not pull this stunt then?"

"There is no stunt." Deborah drew her dressing gown together with both hands, her face impatient. Her shoulder-length blonde hair was ruffled and untidy from her disturbed sleep and she wasn't wearing any make-up. She must look quite a sight, she thought irrelevantly, or rather very relevantly, because Matthew's cold eyes were flicking over her in a way she didn't enjoy.

From the look of him he had been up for some time. Maybe he hadn't slept at all—his manic irritation suggested as much. But he looked fresh enough. He had shaved closely, his dark hair was carefully brushed and he was wearing a very elegantly tailored dark suit. The pale blue shirt striped with broad white stripes, the paisley patterned blue silk tie, emphasised the darkness of those angry blue eyes.

"I don't like being the object of a vendetta."

"You're not the object of a vendetta," Deborah said with mounting irritation. "You're just a stupid idiot!"

He drew a fierce, audible breath. The blue eyes flared. "Well, you're not getting away with it this time," he told her.

"What's that supposed to mean?"

"Just that you'll find out I don't stand still while people pin a donkey's tail on me," he said, moving out of the room at the speed of light.

The door crashed and Deborah put her hands to her aching head. He was the most tiresome man she had ever met! She thought back wistfully to the day she arrived here. She hadn't met him then. Blissful days, she thought. That porter had been right—she shouldn't have ventured out into the mist. Look what she had got herself into now.

CHAPTER FIVE

When Deborah had showered and dressed she put through a call to Hal. He had already heard. He was laughing before she got out a word.

"So that's why you had to have a holiday in Venice. Who'd have suspected it? And I always thought you were a very buttoned-up girl. It just shows—you should never dream up theories about women."

"It isn't true," she said very loudly.

"My eardrums!" Hal groaned. "It must be true. I read it in the papers while I was eating my boiled egg."

His laughter had the low deep rumble of approaching thunder. Hal was in a very jovial mood this morning. Deborah had made his day.

"You mean it's in the English papers too?" That hadn't occurred to her. She was stricken.

Hal relented. "No, not yet. Actually I got a call from Rodney. He's in Rome, remember? He read it there and almost choked on his first cigarette of the day."

Rodney would, she thought bitterly. Wouldn't he just? Always on the spot, especially when you didn't want him. "I didn't know he was in Rome."

"Yes, you did. You never listen, though—always in a tearing hurry to be elsewhere. I sent him over to cover the latest political row. There are elections coming up in a month and someone shot one of the leading Communists.''

"I wouldn't put it past Rodney to do it himself just to get the story,'' Deborah said grimly.

"Nasty! Don't get into a twist,'' said Hal. "Rodney has our interests at heart. He rang to warn me before someone descended on the office.''

"How nice of him! Why do I hate his guts?''

"Because he's got the edge on you,'' said Hal, putting something into his mouth and chewing right into the phone. Deborah took the earpiece away from her ear.

"Do you have to eat doughnuts right into my ear?''

"Crisps,'' said Hal, unabashed. "I need blood sugar.''

"You need shooting! It isn't true, Hal. It's all a mistake—a series of comic accidents,'' she told him.

"I love that,'' Hal roared. "Comic, eh? Rodney described the pictures and I must say they sounded pretty comic to me. An eventful night, I gather.''

"Oh, shut up!'' She slammed the phone down. A lot of help he was. What sort of editor was he, anyway?

Hal rang back a few minutes later. "How about the inside story? You could dictate a few pars to copy.''

"I'm not telling my private life to a giggling copy typist!'' Deborah bellowed. "And it isn't true.''

"No smoke without fire,'' Hal offered.

"That's what makes you a great editor—a profound grasp of the cliché.''

She was getting really angry, and Hal sensed it belatedly. "O.K., what's the story, then?''

Deborah hesitated. "We're just good friends,'' she said lamely.

Hal was still laughing when she slammed the phone down again. When it rang again she snatched it up and said fiercely: "Hal, I swear I'll swing for you one day!"

Rodney's drawling voice murmured: "Where have I heard that before?"

"Oh, it's you, is it? What do you mean by telling Hal all that ridiculous stuff? Why did it have to be you in Rome?"

"I had the good of the paper at heart," Rodney assured her. He was a small, thin man with ginger hair and a precise, self-satisfied expression. He was also a reporter with a nose for news which was second to none. He had a peculiar ability to be invisible. People never noticed Rodney sidling past until it was too late. He picked up stories out of the air. Deborah couldn't stand him and admired him all in one breath. The sight of him made her furious, but his work was far better than her own.

"I bet," she told him bitterly. "Not to mention the good of Rodney Harris."

"You're getting hysterical," Rodney noticed with some evident satisfaction. "Calm down and tell me the real story."

"You mean you don't believe all that stuff in the paper?"

"You forget, I know you. A fortnight ago you were starry-eyed over Robert Langton. Why would you suddenly start an affair with Matthew Tyrell overnight?"

Deborah sighed. She had misjudged Rodney. He wasn't really so bad, after all.

"I only had to give it five minutes' thought and I saw what you were up to," Rodney went on.

"Up to?" Deborah repeated. "What do you mean, up to?"

"Clever girl," Rodney congratulated her. "Frankly, I hadn't expected you to be so devious or so clever. If I were in your shoes that's just what I would have done."

Deborah looked at the phone and shook it as though it had developed a life of its own. "What are you talking about, Rodney?" Her voice had a wary, weary sound.

"You're getting the inside story on Tyrell, right? Sound traditional methods. I didn't think you had it in you. I always had you down as one of those puritanical feminists."

Deborah hung up. She might have known that Rodney would have worked out a corkscrew theory of his own. He was honest, though. That *was* just what Rodney would have done. He had been known to get a story by such underhand means in the past. He wasn't above a little seduction if he thought the occasion warranted it, although why any woman should look twice at him Deborah had never been able to fathom. He had a success rate, though; at least, according to Rodney he did. He had once enlivened a dull weekend in Moscow with a series of anecdotes about his love life. He claimed it was all mathematical. "Like roulette," he explained. "If you keep putting your money on black sooner or later it comes up black. And if you keep trying your luck with women sooner or later one of them says yes."

She had looked at him with loathing. "You nasty little rat!"

"Sticks and stones," he had cooed back at her.

"I object to that statement on behalf of all women." She had been rather under the influence of vodka at the time and her gaze had been very solemn.

"All women dislike the truth. They prefer the fantasy world of romance."

"No wonder you've never got married," she commented. "Who would have you?"

"And why aren't you married?" Rodney had asked, pouring himself another vodka. "Waiting for true love, are we?"

"Drop dead," she had said, and meant it. Rodney was not typical of the men she worked with, but some of his attitudes were all too typical. She knew that the various approaches which had been made to her over the years had been born out of a masculine belief in Rodney's mathematical theory of love. They had all hoped that she would be in the mood to say yes, but she never had, largely because she knew why they were asking and she vigorously objected to their attitude.

Far too often they took the view that sex was another appetite, as easily indulged and as lightly forgotten. Deborah wanted rather more than that from life. She had thought she was getting it from Robert. She had thought he loved her. "Don't take me seriously," he kept saying, and she had been deaf.

Deaf, dumb and blind, she thought, walking out on to her balcony. She felt the stone creaking ominously under her feet and ignored it. Let it break, she thought. What do I care?

The tiny windows in the walls opposite were as blank and guarded as ever. She stared at them, feeling that her life was rather like that—a blank wall with a few tiny windows in it, and all of them barred.

The water this morning had a strange, green depth to it. The sun was striking down into the canal at a peculiar angle. She wondered what it felt like to live at the bottom of the sea or a river and have the bending refractions of

sunlight come filtering down to one in those murky
depths.

For a moment she missed the banging on her door, absorbed in thought. Then she realised what it meant and
went reluctantly to open the door. It was Matthew back
again, the brusque energy of his walk as forceful as ever.
He looked her over in what she felt, irritably, to be an
almost proprietorial fashion.

"Good, you're dressed," he observed.

"What do you want?" she demanded.

"Is that any way to talk to your fiancé?"

For a moment Deborah just stared, open-mouthed.

He gave her a look of sardonic satisfaction. "Got you,
did I?"

"What did you say?"

"You heard." He walked to the window and closed it.
"You weren't out there? The balconies aren't safe.
Didn't they tell you?"

"Yes," she said, brushing the remark aside. "Did you
say fiancé?"

"If they told you, what were you doing out on it? It
could give way any day. Do you want to be killed?"

"At this precise moment I wouldn't give a damn!"

"Defeatist thinking," he said, and she saw suddenly
that he was very pleased with himself. He had a grin from
ear to ear.

"What have you been doing? What are you talking
about fiancés for?"

"I told you I wouldn't let myself be made to look
silly. *Probe* aren't throwing any more of their mud at
me."

Deborah pushed her hands down into the loose white

heavy-knit cardigan she was wearing. "Right, I've got that. Where does the word fiancé come in?"

Matthew pointed at himself with one long finger. Deborah stared, waiting for some other explanation.

"I announced our engagement to the world ten minutes ago," he said smilingly.

"Oh, don't be so ridiculous!"

"You have a very nasty tongue for a lady. I shall expect a little more respect from you in public."

She swallowed, her hands curled into fists in the cardigan pockets. "You aren't serious?" He smiled. "You can't be! You wouldn't do anything so silly and high-handed."

He would. He gave her a sarcastic smile again. "There are more ways than one of skinning a cat."

"Charming!" Deborah felt like a yo-yo being slowly wound up. Any minute she knew she was going to swing wildly into rage. "Now that is just charming. Having got me into the scandal sheets you're now planning to splash me all over the world press, are you? You can think again, Mr. Tyrell! Get on that phone and tell them you changed your mind, there's no engagement."

"For the moment there is," he said, running a hand over his black hair. "Until all the brouhaha dies down we're engaged. In a few weeks you can disappear down whatever dark hole you came out of and I can get on with my life peacefully without you, but until then—we're engaged."

"Not on your life!" Deborah told him with her teeth tightly together. Her jaws ached with tiredness and rage.

"It's my life I'm protecting. I'm not having another of those vicious assassination squads of yours descending on me. I remember the last occasion vividly. They were in the garden of my house, in the basements of my offices, crawling out of inkwells and down chimneys. One bastard even came down the side of my own office in a window-cleaner's cradle and took shots of me at my desk. If I'd had a gun in my drawer I'd have shot him. They questioned my employees, bribed some of them, seduced others..."

Rodney, she thought. For heaven's sake!

"You can call them off," Matthew Tyrell informed her. "Tell them to get off my back or I'll get nasty. I won't have another series of exposé articles about myself in your dreadful rag."

"None were planned," she said in a drained voice. "I promise you."

He laughed shortly.

"I'm telling you the truth! I'm here for one reason only—to have a quiet holiday. I didn't know you were staying here. I'm not chasing you and I don't want to do a story about you. I never did." That was a slight untruth, but she felt justified in telling it.

"I'm afraid I don't believe in the long arm of coincidence," he told her. "As I see it, I was framed last night. You and the *paparazzi* were in cahoots. You came down half-dressed just to get me out there for that second picture. Well, I'm spiking your guns. I don't know exactly what you had in mind as a follow-up to the incriminating pictures, but you can forget it."

"You're a nasty, suspicious, disbelieving swine!" Deborah snapped, and burst into tears.

She sat down on the bed and cried into her fingers, her head bent. She desperately needed sleep. Nobody would listen, even her own editor or one of her colleagues. Robert was in London, she missed him and she loved him, but at this moment she hated him too, and every other man she had ever met. She had bounced from one horrible embarrassment to another for hours, and all because of this man. Now he was landing her with a phoney engagement and he was looking at her with distasteful blue eyes which made her feel small and nasty.

"Oh, my God!" Matthew Tyrell groaned just above her. "Why are women so unspeakable?"

She cried even harder. Her throat was choked with salt and her head ached. She wished she had never set foot in Venice.

"What a rotten trick," Matthew muttered, sitting down beside her and turning her into his chest.

She cried on his shirt, hoping she was ruining it. His tie was smooth and silky on her wet face. He began to stroke her hair as if she was an agitated dog. "Stop it before I burst into tears myself. I can't stand hearing women cry."

"I can't stand men; crying or otherwise," Deborah sniffed into his shirt.

"Oh, you can talk, can you? I thought you were beside yourself with grief, but it was only rage, was it?" He held her away by the shoulders and looked at her without pleasure. "You look as if you're melting. It doesn't suit you to cry."

"I'm not doing it for fun," she muttered, sniffing. A tear ran down her cheek and into the corner of her mouth. She tasted salt on her tongue.

"I only know one thing to do to a woman," said Matthew, and began to do it.

Deborah still felt weak and abandoned and the warm, strong pressure of his mouth was comforting. He drew her down on the bed as he felt the yielding softness of her body in his arms. He was kissing away the tears from eyes, nose, mouth. Deborah lay against him, enjoying it. Her hands were between them. She felt the breathing motion of his chest under the damp shirt. His heart was a steady, powerful rhythm inside the strong rib cage. Deborah pressed her palms against him, feeling the deep inner beating of that heart.

Matthew slid one hand under her cardigan. "How many more layers are there under this?" he asked, disgruntled, as he felt her blouse.

She drew away and eyed him. "I feel better now." She sat up, straightening her clothes.

"Oh, you do?" He lay there, on his back, staring at her. "I begin to get the strong suspicion you're a tease."

"I'm only in Venice for a week—five more days. It seemed far too short when I flew in here and now it seems far too long."

"Come back here," Matthew murmured, putting up a hand to pull her down into his arms.

"Stop that!" Deborah snapped angrily, slapping his hand away.

"Surely I get some privileges as an engaged man? My God, just saying that makes me feel nervous!" He gave an exaggerated shudder. "I've always steered clear of matrimony. I have this antipathy to cages."

"Why on earth did you do it? Are you mad?" She stared at his wry face and Matthew gave her a self-accusing smile.

"I lost my temper. I wasn't going to be hounded by your people again." He wriggled his hand inside her blouse, and Deborah shivered at the cool trail of his fingers up her spine.

"Don't do that!" She slid off the bed and glanced at herself in the dressing-table mirror. Her face was tear-stained, her hair tousled. She went into the little bathroom and bolted the door. When she came out, restored to a cool collected appearance, Matthew was still lying on the bed, his hands linked behind his black head. He had an air of total relaxation, his tie loose, his collar undone.

She looked at him without pleasure. "Don't get comfortable, you're just going."

"Not me," he returned blandly. His eyes flicked over her. "Very fetching," he added in mockery. "How long have you been a journalist?"

"Since I was eighteen."

"And you're twenty-seven," he murmured. "Nine years."

"I can see why you're the head of a multi-national corporation. You've got brains." She wanted to hit him. He looked so totally at his ease, as if he hadn't a care in the world, and Deborah knew that at any moment a tidal wave of curiosity was going to descend on their heads. Matthew Tyrell was a very rich man, a famous man, with a great deal of power. His engagement, particularly with those pictures as background, was going to create a lot of interest.

"Hard-boiled, though," he lamented. "I'm not sure I like that quality in a woman. I like my women to be very feminine, tiny and bewitching, with great big eyes."

"Teresa should have been just up your street, then," she retorted. "You should have got engaged to her."

"I'm beginning to think I should," he nodded. "On the other hand, you're certainly different. I've never met

anyone quite like you and I doubt if I ever will again.''
Before Deborah could decide whether that was meant as
a compliment or not, he added thoughtfully: ''But if I do
I'll run like hell.''

''There's the door, start running,'' she invited hope-
fully.

Matthew smiled, the blue eyes mischievous. ''I'm going to enjoy myself first.''

She gritted her teeth. ''Do you know, I had a feeling
you might say that. But not with me, Mr. Tyrell. That
isn't my scene. I've never been attracted to the high life,
I'm strictly a working girl. So let's stop playing games
and be serious for a moment, shall we?''

''Let's not,'' he said, stretching out a hand in a lazily
commanding gesture. ''Come and join me. I like playing
games, myself.''

''I'm not an enthusiastic games player, I'm afraid.''

''What you need is a little more experience. One snow-
flake doesn't make a blizzard.''

Deborah surveyed him warily. ''Meaning?''

''Just because one man walked out on you it doesn't
mean you have to ignore the whole sex.''

Deborah walked to the window and opened it. The air
had become warm and languid. Autumn was in a suddenly relaxed mood. Sunshine danced along the water and
the sky was a vivid blue.

''Don't go out on the balcony,'' Matthew Tyrell reminded her. ''Taking silly risks won't help.''

''I rather like taking risks. That's why I took up
foreign reporting—I get a kick out of knowing I'm in
slight danger.'' She laughed and gave him a wry look. ''I
have sufficient sense of self-preservation not to want to
get killed. I'm good at looking after myself normally.

I've had a gun pulled on me in the past. I've even been threatened with rape before. It was odd that night when those boys came at me in the mist. Normally I'd have reacted very differently—I've learnt a little judo, I've a good idea how to defend myself.''

"I knew you were a dangerous woman," Matthew observed. "I feel even more grateful for the fact that you didn't actually break my leg when you kicked it."

"I could break your arm," Deborah agreed.

"Please don't. I have a feeling I wouldn't enjoy it."

"It's very painful," she nodded, laughing at him. "The night I got here and went out for a walk in that mist I was in a shattered state. I'd stopped thinking clearly. I was just feeling."

Matthew watched her, his blue eyes intent, not saying anything. She turned away and looked down on the bright canal.

"That's why I screamed when those boys jumped me. All my carefully trained reflexes deserted me. I felt rather foolish about it later."

"Not quite as tough as you'd thought you were?"

She didn't look round, but she heard the smile in his voice and found herself smiling, too.

"Not quite. It was partly the way they acted. They were horribly silent. It wasn't the threat of violence that really got to me, it was the intent in their faces. They were really sinister."

Matthew frowned. "Maybe we should have got the police."

"There was nothing I could tell them. I couldn't even describe the boys. I scarcely looked at their faces. And they didn't do anything. They were going to—I could tell that—but they didn't have the chance, thanks to you."

"I'm glad I happened along," he said.

She shivered. "So am I. I can't tell you how glad."

"It helps to talk about things. If you keep them bottled up they have a tendency to grow, like bulbs kept in a cupboard. Especially something like that." He paused. "And things like the break-up of a love affair."

"That I do not want to talk about." Deborah didn't look at him, her eyes fixed on the sky.

"All the more reason why you should. The thing to do is get him out of your system and talking would help."

"I don't think it would." She had always been far too independent to be ready to tell her life story to anyone at the drop of a hat. In her job one had to be independent. She had only herself to rely on in a tricky situation when she was in a foreign country. Robert had briefly undermined that self-reliant streak in her. He had left her feeling emotionally shaken, uncertain of herself or life, and ever since she arrived in Venice she had been struggling to get back on to an even keel.

"Did you quarrel with him?" asked Matthew.

"Robert isn't the sort of man who quarrels. He's the sort who ducks out on anything so unpleasant." Saying that made it all much clearer in her mind. That was exactly the sort of man Robert was, she realised. It was more complicated than that—Robert was the sort of person who prefers to skate along the surface of life without getting himself too deeply involved in it. He ran from responsibility, especially for other people, and love is a sharing of responsibility. We are always responsible for the happiness of the people we love. Loving is caring, and

Robert didn't have the ability to give that much of himself.

"And he ducked out on you?"

Broken out of her thoughts, she looked at Matthew in sudden, impatient amusement. "You could say that. I fell for him in a big way and he was scared stiff, so he ducked out." She gave him a flushed, defiant stare. "Happy now? Have I told you enough?"

His blue eyes were gentle. "I'm sorry."

"So am I," she admitted wryly. "I don't like feeling a fool."

"I'd noticed that. You've got too much pride, and a little of that goes a long way. Too much of it cuts you off from life altogether."

"You ought to be an editor," Deborah said viciously. "You have the necessary stock of clichés."

"Talking of editors, have you spoken to yours about me today?"

She met his glance and grimaced. "Oh, I've talked to him—when he'd stopped laughing and listened. He'd heard about the pictures and I gathered he couldn't wait to see them. I'll probably find them pinned to the notice-board when I get back to the office. I shall be the laughing stock of the place!"

Matthew's brows drew together slightly. He kept his eyes fixed on her. "Didn't they know what you planned? Or did you dream it up yourself?"

Exasperated, she said: "I didn't plan anything. I keep telling you, but you won't listen. I'm as much a victim as you are—more, if you ask me. You deserve to be chased by the *paparazzi*, but I don't."

Matthew looked at her unreadably, his eyes a very dark

blue. It was impossible to tell if he believed her or
not.

"And I am not going along with this engagement stuff,
either," Deborah added with what she hoped was a con-
vincing firmness. "You don't seem to realise exactly
what effect that would have on my life. I'll be hounded
by my own colleagues!" She thought of Rodney sidling
into her life and trying to wheedle a story out of her. "Being engaged to you would make me news, and I won't
have it!"

For several moments there had been a growing noise
outside the hotel. Deborah had vaguely noticed it, but
now it was becoming quite intrusive. It sounded, she
thought, like a riot. Of course, it couldn't be. Possibly a
whole bus load of new guests had arrived from the airport. She could hear shouting, a buzz of argument, the
shuffle of feet, someone banging on what seemed to be a
door.

The telephone rang and she picked it up. There was an
excited outburst of Italian. "I'm sorry, I don't understand, can you speak English?" she asked.

Matthew rolled over the bed and peremptorily took the
phone out of her hand.

"Do you mind?" she asked, trying to snatch it back.
"That's my phone!"

He was listening, answering whoever it was in brisk
Italian, and he held her away with one hand without difficulty. His brows had drawn together in a straight black
line which deepened the blue of his eyes. Replacing the
phone, he gave her a cool, direct stare.

"I'm afraid it's too late to change my mind. The dogs
of the press are barking outside. They want us to go down

and speak to them and the hotel manager insists that we do. They won't go away until we've given them a statement and pictures. He wants to get rid of them. They're blocking the *riva*."

CHAPTER SIX

DEBORAH had never been on the receiving end of press coverage before, and she felt like a hound who is suddenly being hunted by his own pack. It had taken Matthew fifteen minutes to talk her into coming down with him, and it had only been the hysterical, operatic arrival of the hotel manager which had forced her into agreeing in the end. Waving his arms, the man had begged, threatened, almost wept. The *paparazzi* were infiltrating the kitchens, peering through windows, stopping guests as they left the hotel. He wanted them gone. He wanted his nice, quiet, discreet hotel back the way it had been. All this was delivered in Italian; his English had deserted him in the crisis and only his own mellifluous tongue seemed adequate to convey his desperation. Deborah hadn't understood one word in ten, but she had understood his clasped hands, his wails of reproach. This was, she gathered, a highly respectable hotel. His guests did not like this sort of thing. At this tail end of the season they might desert in droves. Obviously he felt that Deborah and Matthew Tyrell had betrayed him.

She had given in with a weary sigh. Facing her own colleagues, however, she wished she had stood firm.

She did not know any of them, it was true, but how

many times had she been part of their baying pack without considering what it did to someone facing them?

Some were from the *paparazzi*, their cameras clicking away, shouted Italian: "*Bacci*, Signor Tyrell," and hands reaching out to jostle her closer to Matthew for pictures. Others were from English or American papers and she understood everything they said—and wished she didn't.

Despite the entreaty to kiss her, Matthew stolidly ignored the *paparazzi*. He chose which questions he would answer, pretending not to hear others. She saw him in a different light as she stood silently, very flushed and angry, beside him.

The amusing, casual companion she had come to know in the two days of their acquaintance had vanished. The man standing next to her was the head of a multi-national corporation and he had undergone a transformation in personality. His voice was cool and clipped. His face had a hard watchful shrewdness and the blue eyes were expressionless.

Listening to him parrying questions, fencing lightly without making any slipshod, incautious answers, she could see that she scarcely knew him at all. She had only seen the tip of the iceberg, and now here was the iceberg in person, revealed in glacial blandness. Without realising it, she had been wondering what sort of businessman Matthew was—this man whose temper could flare and sink in a moment, who talked easily and with charm, could laugh at himself and other people without being trivial. She had to recognise now that he was more impressive than she had realised. He had an air of calm authority as he talked. He didn't allow anyone to hustle him, nor did he snap or lose his temper now.

"Just leave it all to me," he had told her, and Deborah did just that. She refused to say a word. She let Matthew do all the talking.

Some of the questions were very revealing. "Is your friendship with Leila Montrey over, Mr. Tyrell?" an American asked. "Does she know about Miss Linton?"

That was one Matthew chose to ignore. Deborah didn't look at him, but she felt her flush deepen. The name meant nothing to her, but she wasn't blind to the implications. It hadn't occurred to her that all this might embarrass Matthew in that sort of way. She had vague memories of his supposed love life from the *Probe* investigation four years earlier, but that side of his activities hadn't really been what she had been concentrating on at the time. Her part of that story had largely been to check on the research establishments his firm owned. She hadn't met or even seen Matthew himself, and although Rodney had several times expressed the opinion that Matthew Tyrell had it made she hadn't taken much notice.

Rodney, of course, would envy Matthew. "What a track record!" he had sighed. "I wish I had his pulling power." Rodney believed firmly that all women were impressed by money. He always drove flashy cars because he imagined they would increase his desirability. He spent money freely on dates and expected a return for it. Rodney had a very materialistic mind. Any girl who went out with him knew what he would expect in exchange for the good food and wine he was giving her.

If she turned him down after that sort of expense, he crossed her name off his list.

Deborah wondered if that was how Matthew Tyrell operated, too. He wouldn't need to be so crudely obvious, of course. Or so insistent.

A man of his background and money wouldn't need to do the hunting; he would be too busy running.

"How long have you known each other?" someone shouted.

Matthew said: "Long enough," and they all laughed. Several of them looked at Deborah in a way she found infuriating. She felt like kicking them and Matthew gave her a quick, sidelong look which held amusement. He knew her well enough by now to know what was in her mind, she realised. There was a little glint in the blue eyes. Maybe she had, without being aware of it, some special expression when she was feeling like hitting out at someone, and Matthew was beginning to recognise it.

"Where did you meet?"

"When's the wedding date?"

Matthew parried those without difficulty, as he had the other personal questions which Deborah had found breathtakingly insolent but which he took without a sign of surprise or anger. Once or twice she caught a cold hardness entering his face, but he banished it without apparent struggle.

At last he cut the pack short. "That's it, gentlemen." He put an arm around Deborah and despite the excited attempts to take more pictures, ask more questions, he managed to force her back into the hotel. The hall porter slammed the doors in the faces of the press, who howled through the glass in a last desperate attempt to enter. Convinced their quarry had no intention of coming out again, though, they soon rushed off to phone in stories or get film developed and mounted on blocks.

"A charming profession you've got," Matthew commented, giving her a wry smile. "Minds like rats in a maze. They just keep going along blind alleys without having a clue where they're going."

"Oh, they know," Deborah told him. "You don't seem to realise—there's an editor sitting in an office waiting for them and if they don't bring back the right story they'll get their heads bitten off."

"Now that would be an improvement with some of them."

"You're just prejudiced," she said, automatically defending her own despite the embarrassed fury she had been feeling earlier.

He gave her a glance which was full of that ironic amusement she was beginning to know as typical of him. "Do you know, I had the distinct impression out there that you weren't over-enamoured of them, either."

She bit back a smile. He was far too shrewd. Even more maddening, she knew he had seen the beginning of the smile. His eyes mocked her as she tried to tighten her lips to hide it.

"Not, of course, that you would admit to any such thing."

"You only see them from your side of the fence," she pointed out.

"And a pretty horrific sight they are," he agreed.

"They're human, too."

"I'd need evidence of that." He was looking at her

with his lids half down over his eyes. "Starting with yourself, perhaps." Before she could take in what he meant by that or react he had walked away to where the hotel manager and the hall porter were having a whispered conference in stage Italian, their hands gesticulating, the voices pointedly audible although intended to convey secrecy.

Matthew had a short conversation with the hotel manager. Deborah didn't take in any of it, since she was grappling with the implication of what he had just said and furiously deciding that if he dropped any similar hints in future she would definitely break his arm. If he thought she was starting a fling with him just because they had been thrown together by circumstance, he could think again!

She would show him how human she was if he tried any of his experienced seduction scenes again!

He returned, poker-faced, and urged her into the lift. It rose with the rattle of chains which always accompanied its movements. From the foyer the hotel manager and the hall porter gazed after them with disapproval. Deborah could see what they thought. From the way they eyed her she had scarlet woman written all over her. She found it so irritating she felt like screaming.

"Go and pack," said Matthew, watching her. "We're getting out of here before the *paparazzi* get back." His mouth twisted wryly. "And they'll be back when their cameras are reloaded."

"I'm getting the first plane back to London," Deborah advised him. That idea had occurred to her while she was listening to the press bellowing questions.

The most sensible thing they could do now was to vanish in opposite directions—a divided target is harder to hit. She knew her own profession—there is nothing so dead as yesterday's news. They would soon cease to be of interest to the papers. All they had to do was lie low for a few days. She realised that she was going to get a lot of teasing when she got back to her own newspaper. People there were going to laugh whenever they saw her. But the main thing at the moment was to get out of the limelight.

Matthew didn't blink an eyelash. Although she had spoken with casual confidence of going back to London, Deborah was relieved that he hadn't argued. She had had a feeling he wouldn't let her go, although what he could do to stop her she didn't know. And why should he, anyway? It was all so stupid. If he had wanted to spike *Probe*'s guns over those pictures of them he had done that now. *Probe* couldn't have made anything out of it, even if they had been behind the *paparazzi*, as he imagined. Matthew had given it all a totally new twist now. Their pretended engagement made it all look far more romantic, respectable.

When the lift stopped at his floor with that little jerk he pulled open the gate and stood there looking calmly at her. "I've arranged for us to go out the back way. There's a side gate which, with luck, will have escaped the attention of the *paparazzi*."

"Nothing escapes their attention," she said wearily. "Especially side gates and back entries—believe me."

"Oh, I do."

"I'm sure you do."

They stared at each other and giving her a grin Matthew said: "All the same, we'll try our luck that way. I'm arranging for a diversionary tactic out at the *riva* entrance."

"Get one of your girl-friends to do a strip," Deborah muttered.

"Excellent idea," he returned blandly. "If you'll join me when you've packed the hotel manager will have made the arrangements. See you in the foyer in half an hour."

She had just finished packing when Andrea rang. The international line crackled and fizzed, making it hard to hear exactly what she was shrieking, but Deborah didn't need to hear the words. She could hear the intonation.

"Andrea, I can't talk now."

Shriek, shriek! Andrea came back unintelligibly.

"I'll ring you tomorrow," Deborah shouted very slowly, pausing between each word. Making a noise like a deep sea diver, Andrea tried to answer, but Deborah shouted, "Goodbye," and hung up. She did not feel she had the energy to try to communicate at long distance with her sister at this moment.

It should have occurred to her that sooner or later Andrea would hear all about it. Perhaps the English newspapers had been on to her. Looking at herself with dry comprehension in the mirror as she brushed her hair, Deborah thought: probably *Probe* has been probing away like mad. Hal would have no scruples about using their own team on her. A story was a story, and the way this one was developing she really couldn't even blame him. In his shoes no doubt she would make the same decisions. Hal's thinking was perfectly clear to her: if *Probe* didn't do the story, someone else would.

In this case, no doubt everyone else would. She herself might not be of any particular interest to readers, but Matthew Tyrell certainly was, and his activities were bound to attract attention. *Probe* wouldn't dare to miss out just because Deborah was one of their own people. Far more likely, they would try to wheedle her into giving them an exclusive.

The porter arrived a moment later to take her case down. He was polite in an icy fashion and Deborah followed him, her face resigned. It was an interesting experience to be labelled a scarlet woman, no doubt, but one which she was not particularly enjoying.

Matthew was waiting for her. "Your case will be sent on," he told her. "We're going to have to walk along some back alleys and you may need to run, and the cases would just hamper us."

"Have you arranged your diversion?"

"Yes. They'll expect us to go out on to the *riva*. I've sent for a gondola. That should keep them out there, waiting for us to try to make a dash for it along the canals."

Deborah wasn't convinced. "They'll post someone at the back—I know I would. Always cover all exits."

"I'd thought of that," Matthew returned with calm amusement.

She did not ask what he meant; she felt she preferred not to know. She discovered, anyway. As they emerged from the back of the hotel she saw a young man in a blue shirt stiffen eagerly. He had bloodhound written all over him. Before he could alert his colleagues, however, two burly men in rolled shirtsleeves pounced on him. Pinned between them he was helpless to do more than shout.

"Run!" Matthew commanded.

He grabbed Deborah's hand. She broke into a run beside him up the narrow, shadowy alley leading from the back of the hotel. After that she lost track of where they went. They raced along past high, dark walls festooned with washing. Women looked at them with indifferent eyes as they brushed their way past. Venice was a honeycomb of maze-like alleys behind the open stateliness of the public buildings. They tore up steps which were worn by generations of feet. They darted over narrow crumbling bridges. Matthew seemed to know his way, but Deborah was lost within moments.

"Can we slow down?" she gasped. "My lungs are giving out!"

He looked round at her and slowed. "You're not in very good shape, are you, then?"

Puffing, she leaned on a cracked stone wall. "Another minute and I'd be a hospital case!"

Irritatingly his breathing was almost as regular as normal. He stood beside her, listening for sounds of pursuit, but none came.

"I think we've shaken them off," he said.

"Thank God for that! I hope it doesn't occur to them to watch the airport."

"Of course it will, but they can watch it until they're blue in the face. We won't be going there."

"I am," said Deborah, at once.

"No, you're not. They'd tear you limb from limb. I've got a car waiting two minutes from here."

"I'm going home," Deborah insisted, as Matthew's long fingers closed round her arm, urging her away from the wall. "I'm going back to London today."

Matthew hustled her along without actual violence. He didn't bother to argue.

"I am," Deborah repeated on a note of shaken insistence. She did not like the way he didn't answer. He looked far too cool.

"I want to go to the airport," she said as Matthew put her into the waiting car a few moments later.

The driver started the ignition and the car slid smoothly away. The windows had smoked glass in them and Deborah wondered if it was bullet-proof. It looked like the sort of car which would have bullet-proof windows. She wondered if it had been made for the Mafia. It was both luxurious and streamlined, just the sort of car for Matthew Tyrell, she decided, looking at him with mounting irritation. "I want to go to the airport," she said again.

"Change the record," Matthew murmured. "You've already made your point and I've explained why you can't catch a plane home at once."

"Where are you taking me? You're not shanghai-ing me, Mr. Tyrell. Just stop this car and let me out." She wrenched at the door handle impotently.

"It's locked from the dashboard," Matthew informed her kindly.

Deborah said something explosive.

"When you're in a temper you get little red lights in your eyes," Matthew said unflatteringly. "I had a pet rat when I was a boy that looked like that."

Deborah took a long breath, her hands curling into fists.

"Don't hit me," Matthew mocked. "I need both my arms."

Before she had a chance to realise what that meant he was demonstrating the meaning in a very practical way. The driver gazed stolidly in front of him.

Deborah had been taken off guard. Before she could push him away or protest, Matthew had one arm locked round her. His free hand tilted her chin, his fingers along her cheek. She glared at him momentarily before his mouth came down against her lips.

He was amused as he coaxed her lips apart. She could feel the slight tremor in the warm outline of his mouth moving against her own and her anger flared out of all control. He was laughing at her—that stung. She was still sensitive after the humiliation of discovering her mistake over Robert. No man was laughing at her, she thought, trying to twist herself out of his grip. Having failed to manage that, she tried to kick him as she had before and merely found his knee firmly anchoring her against the seat. It was an undignified and infuriating little struggle, and it ended because Matthew suddenly lost his temper.

The hand round her chin tightened like a vise and he began to kiss her without amusement, very hard. For a few seconds the pressure of his lips was resisted. Deborah couldn't work out afterwards what had happened to her. At the time all she knew was that blood began singing in her ears. She couldn't hear anything through it. Her body went limp, yielding to the hand at her back which was forcing her towards Matthew. Her skin grew hot. From resisting his mouth she began meeting it with fierce response, her hands flying up to frame his head between them, his thick hair prickling against her palms.

Matthew pulled back and looked at her. She hadn't even been aware until then that she had shut her eyes. Now she opened them to stare at him in consternation.

He looked quite different. There was a flush along his cheekbones and his eyes were gleaming. Looking into them, Deborah had no difficulty in recognising their expression. Excitement, triumph, a trace of self-satisfaction—it all lay there for her to read for a few seconds before Matthew hurriedly blanked it all out. Matthew Tyrell was a dangerous man, Deborah realised. Any man who could disguise sheer bullet-headed determination to get his own way under a bland façade was dangerous.

His one weakness, she imagined, was his temper. It was the one crack in the façade. She had wondered about the casual, relaxed charm which somehow did not seem to fit in with his public persona. He might have a lot of lady friends, but he was also, she remembered from her research into him, a tough member of a very tough profession.

She looked angrily into the blue eyes. "I don't like being grabbed, Mr. Tyrell!"

"I'm your fiancé, remember," he mocked.

"I wish you'd stop saying that! It isn't true, and I want you to let the whole ridiculous notion drop out of sight."

"In due course," he murmured, settling back into his seat, his long legs stretched out in front of him and an air of extremely pleasurable anticipation about him. Deborah looked at him irritably, not liking the smile he wore.

"I must have been crazy to play along with you so far. You talked me into it."

"I'm very persuasive," Matthew agreed, laughing under his breath, and she didn't like the way he laughed any more than she had liked the way he smiled.

The back of her neck prickling, she snapped: "Just don't get any ideas, Mr. Tyrell!"

"Too late," he admitted coolly. "I've already got them. I've been fascinated by blonds with big green eyes for years, particularly when they have figures like yours. You really should have been a model, you have a very enticing way of walking."

Pink ran up her face. Furiously she snapped: "You can forget ideas like that: I'm not interested."

"All the better," he drawled, watching her with that infuriating mixture of amusement and patience. "I've never enjoyed hunting a tame quarry."

"You're making me very angry, Mr. Tyrell," Deborah said through her teeth, conscious of a deep burning flush.

He laughed softly. "So I see. I like the way your eyes spit sparks when you're cross. I can't wait to see what happens when you dissolve into my arms."

Deborah drew a long breath. She counted to ten before she said with assumed calm: "I see. That's what I'm going to do, is it? Nice of you to warn me! I like to have an inkling of what's going on inside a man's head when he grabs me as though I were a doll in a toyshop."

Matthew's eyes glinted with amusement. "You mean you didn't know? Then maybe it's high time you found out. You've been missing out."

"Not in my book," Deborah said tersely. She looked out of the car window and watched the landscape. The nerve of the man! she thought. How dared he talk about her like that?

"Where are we going?" she asked without turning round, her eyes on the flat green vineyards through which they were driving.

"A friend of mine has a villa in the Dolomites. He's lent it to us for a couple of days."

Deborah bristled. "Oh, no," she said. "No, you don't! I'm not spending two days with you in a villa anywhere, so forget it."

"This is Trevire," Matthew drawled. "Bassano is half an hour's drive from here and the villa is some miles from Bassano."

"I don't need a geography lesson. I just want to be taken back to Venice to catch a plane to London."

"The scenery is quite magnificent from the villa," he told her.

"I mean it. Take me back to Venice!"

"Don't be tiresome." Matthew folded his arms and settled himself in a more comfortable position. "I'm dog tired. I'm going to have a nap. Wake me up when we get to the villa."

She didn't believe he meant it—until, turning after a moment with a fresh volley of angry complaint on her tongue, she was silenced to discover that he was fast asleep. It was not pretence. His whole face had relaxed into gentle lines. She watched him incredulously. How on earth had he managed to do that? Although she was used to sleeping at all hours of the day and night it always took her some time to get to sleep during the day and, even then, she had to have a darkened room to do it in. She couldn't imagine falling asleep in a car in broad daylight like someone snapping off a light.

She didn't have the heart to shake Matthew awake. For a few moments she watched him, probing the lean planes of his face without discovering anything more about him than she already knew. Even in sleep, Matthew Tyrell's face had some way of keeping its secrets.

The car sped on into the lower foothills of the Dolomites. Above them the deep green of pines bristled against the sky. The air grew clearer, sharper. They took a road which wound upwards between the pines. A few houses showed between the trees, their walls cracked and shabby but comfortably merging with their surroundings. They looked as if they had been there for hundreds of years, yet they were perched on the dry, stony sides of the hills as if about to slide down into the valley. A few chickens scratched among the olives and cypresses which were round the houses. Somehow there was a desultory air about the whole landscape. It looked temporary and seemed to have been looking like that for as long as could be remembered. The dramatic flourish it had had from a distance evaporated as one came closer and noticed the poverty of the soil, the decay of the houses.

When the car swung in at an open gate Deborah sat up. She didn't make a sound, but Matthew neatly woke up, stretching.

"I wish I knew how you did that," Deborah complained. "I could do with some sleep myself, but I've never been able to cat nap at a moment's notice."

"You should learn. It's very useful." Matthew glanced out of the window as they bumped along a narrow grassy track.

"We're at this villa, I suppose," said Deborah.

"This must be murder on the springs." They were bouncing about like a dodgem car at a fair.

Through a grove of olives they saw the little house. White, gabled, it nestled against the side of the hill in a nervous fashion as if ready to grab hold of a tree if it began to slide. It was not very big, Deborah noticed. Three or four rooms, at the most, she imagined. Maybe it had been a farmhouse. The framewood of the structure looked as if it had been run up in a hurry.

"I'm not staying here alone with you," she said on a spurt of fresh anger.

Matthew was staring out of the car window. "It doesn't look as if we're going to be alone."

Deborah looked out, too, and gave a little groan. Teresa Scalatio was standing on the long wooden verandah fronting the villa.

CHAPTER SEVEN

THERE was no mistaking Teresa's attitude as they emerged from the car. She ran towards Matthew, drama in her face, already beginning to give him her views in excited Italian. Her dark eyes flashed at Deborah with loathing just once before returning to Matthew. He held her off as if she were a difficult child, his hands clasping her shoulders.

"Behave yourself! You know Deborah doesn't understand your language. And what are you doing here?"

"Papa told me he had lent you the little villa." She wriggled her slender shoulders in an attempt to escape his grasp. "Matt, how could you? When I saw those photos I wept and wept. She is your mistress. I didn't believe it until I saw them." Her English, like her father's, was strongly accented but very good and had a transatlantic flavour. "I hate you!" She said that with sighing emphasis, her enormous eyes eating him, making it clear she did not mean a word of it.

"Papa had no business telling you anything." Matthew looked at her with indulgent impatience. "It was you who tipped off the *paparazzi*, I suppose. Not a very nice thing to do, was it?"

Her apricot cheeks flushed most becomingly. She chewed on her lower lip, looking down. "I . . ."

"Don't lie," Matthew ordered drily.

Teresa looked at him through lowered black eyelashes, pouting. "It was probably *her*. They said in the paper that she's a reporter."

"You need spanking," Matthew told her. "And I'm just the man to do it if you tell me any more lies. You're a very naughty little girl."

"Little girl?" Insult gave the dark eyes added depth. "I'm not a little girl, I'm a woman." She eyed him languorously. "You refuse to admit it, that's all. Others aren't so slow to see it."

"Shameless hussy!" There was that amusement in his face again. Deborah could see that, for all his avoidance of her, he found Teresa charming, especially this afternoon. The girl was wearing a cherry red sweater with a becomingly deep cleavage, a wide tight belt pulling in her waist, her skirt a full circle as she moved back to detach herself from him, the swish of it drawing attention to her slim legs.

"How did you come to know any of the *paparazzi*?" Matthew demanded.

For a few seconds she hesitated, then she shrugged crossly. "Gianni took some pictures of me last summer. We dated a few times."

"Does your father know that?" Matthew eyed her with cynicism. She didn't answer. "I thought not," he added, his mouth quirking. "He wouldn't like it, would he?"

"Gianni doesn't think I'm a little girl," Teresa said with a quick, flirtatious look.

"Then you stick with him," said Matthew in what

Deborah felt to be a rather heartless fashion, his eyes amused.

Teresa stamped her foot. "Oh! Gianni is right—you are a bastard!"

Unperturbed, Matthew nodded. "Gianni is absolutely right: I am. So get off back to Venice and don't let me see you here again or I may well give you that spanking which your father should have delivered a long time ago."

"You wouldn't dare!" Half enraged, half excited, she dared him with her black eyes, quivering from head to foot.

Matthew took one step, the smile leaving his face. Teresa met the dangerous hard blue eyes and fled down the steps. She turned at bay, spitting like a little cat.

"Bastard, bastard!"

Matthew shot forward and she retreated at top speed, running like a deer until she was lost in the olive trees.

"How will she get back to Venice?" Deborah asked, feeling rather worried about her.

"She got here," Matthew said indifferently. "She can get back."

Deborah regarded him with dislike. "She's right and so is Gianni—you are a bastard."

The smile was back in his eyes. "I'm a realist. I suggest you try it some time."

He unlocked the villa front door and Deborah gingerly followed him into the hall. She glanced around her with curiosity. The floor was tiled in a brilliant blue and white ceramic design which threw back the light falling from the open door. The walls were white and very closely covered with a series of sketches of the sea, small framed charcoal impressions.

Through the open door she heard the engine of the car and spun. "He's going!" She raced back outside, waving. The driver did not look back. Deborah watched the vehicle disappear and felt like screaming.

Marching back into the house, she found Matthew had vanished. "Where are you? Where's the car gone? I'm not staying here, not with you!" She looked in at the nearest door. The room was empty. She took in the bamboo furniture, the glass-topped table and the great brassbound green tub in which a rubber tree stood with an air of lurking menace like a fugitive from the jungle. "Where are you?" she demanded, moving away.

Matthew appeared at another door. "You can have this room."

Deborah joined him and looked over his shoulder at the bed with its flower-sprigged sheets and continental quilt. "That's what you think! I'm going back to Venice."

"Not in those shoes," Matthew said tolerantly. "You'd never make it. Those shoes weren't made for walking." He swung the door back, his hand at the handle. "A bolt, see? You can retreat in here and feel secure whenever you like."

"Why are you so obstinate?" she wailed.

"I'm not obstinate," he argued. "I just know that my way of doing things is right. There's a difference."

"Not to the naked eye. From my angle it looks like sheer pigheaded love of your own way."

"That, too," he agreed. "My room, you'll be relieved to hear, is on the other side of the hall."

"Good," she retorted. "Stay in it."

"That's up to you," he said, cool as a cucumber, and wandered away, but not before the blue eyes had mocked her briefly. Deborah stared after his black head, feeling her heart knock wildly under her ribs. The nerve of the man, she thought, trying to whip up anger. What did he mean by that? Did he really imagine she might invite him. . . She broke off that thought, her colour deepening. Yes, he did. Well, he could think again!

"I'm starving," she said frostily, following him. "I suppose there isn't any food."

"Now why should you suppose that?"

"Where is it, then?"

"Where do you usually find food?" She looked at him in muted irritation and he added with that maddening air of kind amusement, "Try the kitchen."

Bristling, Deborah asked: "Who's doing the cooking?"

"Well, it isn't me," Matthew shrugged. "You're hungry. You do it."

He went into the room on the other side of the hall. Deborah glared at the back of him, then turned and went off to search for the kitchen. It was the only other room, and it was far and away the largest. Sunny, spacious, it had waxed wood furniture and every modern gadget, all of them kept in pristine condition, shiny and inviting. She wondered what use this villa got—how often did the Scalatio family come here? Money had been spent making this isolated little place a luxurious home, yet it looked unlived in, unloved. Presumably they kept it as a holiday home. What a waste, Deborah thought, opening the deep freeze cabinet which took up a vast amount of space along one wall.

She did not have time to wait for meat to thaw, so she sorted through the branded frozen food and chose items which could be cooked from frozen. The cooker was electric. Five minutes later she was already at work, the smell of cooking on the air.

Matthew came when she called a quarter of an hour later. "My God, you're a fast worker," he commented, staring at the table.

"Sit down and eat it while it's hot." She was flushed, which might have been due to having been so busy, but which she knew very well was due instead to an increasing nervousness about being alone with Matthew Tyrell in this place.

One side of the kitchen was occupied by a pinewood table and chairs. Matthew took one of the chairs and Deborah sat opposite. "It isn't the sort of gourmet cooking you're used to, I suppose, but it was the best I could do under the circumstances."

"It smells delicious," he said, beginning to eat. "Scalatio told me there was wine in the cellar, but we'll leave that for later."

Deborah stiffened. "We'll leave it altogether."

He shot her a look, grinning. "Afraid it will lead to a seduction scene?"

"Not with me," she assured him.

"You're too optimistic."

Her colour rose higher. "If you think . . ."

"Yes?" He was laughing under his breath and she seethed, staring at him.

"Not on your life," she said firmly.

"We're here for a couple of days, at least, and we've got to find some way of passing the time. I don't know a more enjoyable way of filling in time, do you?''

"There's a lot more to life than jumping in and out of bed," Deborah said scornfully.

"I knew it—you're repressed."

"I am not! Don't bother to spin that old line to me. I was seventeen when I first heard it, and I didn't believe it then. Men always try to convince you that if you won't go to bed with them it's because you're repressed. They can't seem to believe that for a woman sex is always an expression of love, not an appetite.''

Matthew surveyed her coolly. "I don't think of sex as an appetite."

"No?" She smiled contemptuously at him.

"No. A game, maybe, a very pleasant game for two."

Deborah laughed angrily. "Oh, that's another variation of the same theme. I've heard that line before, too. And it's just as despicable. Love's neither an appetite nor a game. It's far more serious than either.'' She pushed away her half-finished meal and stood up, looking at him with furious eyes. "Keep your hands to yourself while we're here or I'll lose my temper, Mr. Tyrell!"

She walked out in a sudden silence. She could feel him staring after her, but he seemed to have nothing to say. Deborah went out into the cool autumn sunshine and looked around her with a caged feeling of desperation. The dry hillsides folded on each other in warm, rolling curves. The olive trees rustled in the faint wind.

Robert thought of love as a game and when he realised she had taken his game seriously he had fled. Looking back over her years in journalism she could not even remember how many times men had tried to talk her into bed with one or other variation of the theme that sex was just another part of life and she was missing out if she refused to give them what they wanted. At times she had almost begun to believe it herself, but somehow her intelligence had refused to let her start to think like that. Love was too important to be treated so lightly. It was the driving force that created life itself, and to misuse it was insanity.

She envied her sister because Andrea was deeply embedded in her life. For all her little complaints, Andrea had all she wanted. Her husband and children loved and needed her, and Andrea knew it. It is not in human nature to be content all the time. A divine discontent constantly bubbles up inside us, making us reach out for something we feel we have not got, but deep down inside herself Andrea would not really have changed a thing in her world. She just liked to look outside it now and then and wonder what it was like to be someone else.

Deborah walked along the terrace and picked her way over the stony earth beneath the trees, their shifting shadow moving with the wind.

She had once thought her career would give her all she wanted, but Robert had taught her she was fooling herself. He had hurt her unbearably when he rejected the depth of her feelings for him. Robert preferred to think of love as a game, and she had mistaken the colour of his mind. He was not the man she had thought he was—and facing that she now realised that she had loved someone who did not exist. Robert had been an illusion.

I'm a fool, she thought. Only a complete idiot would

fall in love with someone who doesn't exist. If Robert hurt me, I asked for it. I threw myself into love without looking where I was going. How many times has Hal warned me against leaping before I look? It's my character again—I rush into things. After years of holding men at bay she had run headlong into Robert's arms because she had begun to think she would never know what it was like to love and be loved. She had chosen to love Robert because she believed he cared for her. However lightheartedly and selfishly men see love, women have a deeper intuition. Love is the secret of life, and women are born knowing it.

Did I really love him at all? she asked herself. If it was illusion then this pain is not wounded love—it's wounded self-esteem. I was humilitated by realising that I'd made a fool of myself. I created the man I told myself I loved. I wasn't in love with Robert; I was in love with love itself.

A stone rattled past her and she spun. Matthew had walked up without her noticing his approach. He looked at her calmly, placing a hand against the gnarled trunk of one of the trees and leaning there, his body a graceful arc unconscious of itself, the line of chest, waist, hip disposed elegantly.

"I apologise. I deserved that little kick in the teeth. Consider me suitably chastened."

For some reason that made her feel worse. She turned away, her head bent, stifling a harsh sob.

"Don't," said Matthew, moving away from the tree.

Deborah was struggling to keep tears at bay. She felt she was in need of tears. Her feelings were in violent turmoil; they needed the release of childish weeping.

She stuffed her hand into her mouth, biting the knuckles.

"Oh, hell," Matthew groaned, turning her into his arms. "Not tears again! I told you, I can't stand hearing women cry."

"Don't make them cry, then," she muttered into his chest. He had a comforting strength, the warmth of his body enfolding her as his arms went round her, the hardness of his muscles enforced by masculinity yet tempered with a wry gentleness as he began to stroke her hair.

"I'm a swine. Go on, say it."

"You're a swine," Deborah whispered chokily.

He laughed. She felt his chest heaving under her face. "You take me too literally."

"I don't want to take you at all." She felt stronger now. There was something very reassuring about his voice when he spoke like that. It put new life into her. She lifted her face and tried to move away.

"Stay there," ordered Matthew, his voice faintly husky. "I like having you leaning on me. You're a strange mixture of assured career woman and femininity. I'm never sure whether you're going to launch yourself at me like Wonder Woman or dissolve into helpless tears like a little girl."

Deborah couldn't help laughing. His blue eyes were coaxing, teasing. "Unpredictability is my chief charm," she agreed.

"I'm glad we agree on something," said Matthew with mockery. He produced a hankie and began to dry her face. She stood meekly letting him do it, finding it very enjoyable. When he had finished he kissed her lightly on the nose.

"Forgive me?"

"Do I have your promise not to talk like that again?"

He considered the request, mouth wry. "Do I have to? I agree I'd never looked at it from your point of view, but have you tried looking at it from mine? I'm a man, and when I see something I fancy my instinct is to reach out and grab it."

"Try controlling your instincts," she advised seriously.

"That takes half the fun out of life."

"It may be fun to you, but it can be a bore to a woman," Deborah told him, prickling again. "How would you like to be bombarded with remarks like that? I work with men all the time, frequently abroad, where we're thrown into each other's company for hours at a time. I'm sick to the back teeth with getting that sort of proposition from men I only know slightly. What makes you all think that you're God's gift to women? What makes you think it's any compliment to be treated like a disposable hankie?" Her face had flushed again and she was boiling over with rage.

"Hey," Matthew interrupted, his own flashpoint suddenly reached. "I wasn't. . . ."

"Oh, yes, you were. Just because we were alone in that house you thought I'd fall into your arms without a murmur. Well, you can think again!"

"Oh, can I?"

Deborah stiffened, looking up at his face. Hard, angry blue eyes stared down at her. When she tried to move away she found his arm barring escape, tight against her back.

"Your trouble is, you take life a damned sight too

seriously," Matthew informed her through his teeth. "It's time you learnt how to give in a little."

"Not to you—" Deborah began, and got no further.

His head came down so swiftly she had no chance to elude him. She caught one quick glimpse of his eyes—it made her stomach tighten in shock. Passion burnt in them, a passion she had seen once before in his eyes. Matthew's game had turned serious in a flash and it left Deborah oddly weak to see that expression in his face.

Her lips parted helplessly under the erotic demand of his mouth. She was pulled close to his body, forcibly made aware of the hard length of his thigh, the hand at her back sliding upward, moulding her sensuously into a yielding curve. The intimacy of their touching bodies lit something deep inside her. Her hands clung to his shoulders, her mouth beginning to quiver into an urgent response. She heard Matthew groan huskily, then his hand moved lightly. As it closed over the upward tilt of her breast Deborah's whole body began to burn. Desire ran through her so fast she had no time to consider what was happening to her. She buried her hands in Matthew's thick hair, trembling, abandoned to the fierce, sweet feeling.

Matthew broke off the kiss a moment later, breathing roughly. He held her, looking down into her overheated face, and Deborah couldn't meet his eyes. She couldn't stop shaking, either.

"You were saying?" Matthew asked mockingly.

Deborah pulled herself together. Wrenching herself out of his arms, she gave him a brief, furious glare.

"Go to hell!" Turning to run, she tripped over an exposed root and only saved herself from a humiliating fall by catching at one of the trees. Matthew shot forward, but she had already straightened. She gave him one more look, contempt and loathing in it, then walked away with more dignity, her head held high. He should have shrivelled on the spot by this stately exit, but she heard him laughing, which only made her angrier.

Inside the villa she stood in the quiet, blue and white tiled hall, listening to the silence and wondering what on earth had happened to her out there in Matthew Tyrell's arms.

After all her protests she had been only too responsive. She despised herself. Now he would think he only had to pile on the pressure to have her give way completely.

She went into her own room and bolted the door. Sitting on the bed, she contemplated her position with alarm. Alone with him out here, she was like a tethered goat alone with a tiger. Sooner or later he was going to make a serious attempt to get her into bed, and after what had just happened between them Deborah no longer felt absolutely sure of her own ability to keep him at arms length.

She was vulnerable at the moment, although it had only just come home to her how vulnerable. She had imagined that her disillusion over Robert would make it impossible for her to react like that to another man, but perhaps her very unhappiness had fuelled the sudden wave of sexual desire which had risen inside her.

It had been obvious to her for some time that she liked Matthew Tyrell, maddening though he might be at times. He was very attractive. She felt awake and alive in his company. Their minds sparked whenever they were together. Now she had to admit, however reluctantly, that it wasn't just their minds which sparked. She was physically aware of him too, and she had had to realise that Matthew was physically aware of her.

All that didn't add up to love, of course. It was a small and simple equation and she knew the answer. Matthew had told her frankly. He fancied her.

She looked across the room at the little white dressing-table which was set into a fitted bedroom unit taking up one wall of the room. Her flushed, disturbed face stared back. Her blonde hair was ruffled, her nose rather shiny, her lipstick almost non-existent. God knows why Matthew should fancy her, looking like that. Men were funny creatures. In the past she had often thought that they pursued anything which ran away—hunters by nature. No doubt Robert would have taken her more seriously if she had started running. Matthew had only lost his temper just now because she had challenged him, however unconsciously.

Men's egos were unstable things, liable to get out of hand if anyone handled them roughly. Matthew had been quite reasonable until he suddenly felt she was issuing a challenge. At once he had taken it up and she regretted ever having lost her own temper enough to make him lose his.

She knew better now. In future she would keep the temperature very low, not so much because she was frightened of him as because she was rather worried about herself.

She lay down on the bed, abruptly tired. It had been a long and worrying day. Matthew had managed that catnap in the car, but Deborah had been awake for what seemed like a week.

She closed her eyes, stretching. This time next year I probably won't even remember what Robert looked like, she told herself. Time heals everything. It was doing its healing job now, delicately weaving fresh skin over the open wound Robert had left in her emotions. Matthew Tyrell had helped, of course. Hard to brood miserably with that man rushing you from pillar to post. One thing, Deborah told herself sleepily—he's never boring. Anything else, but not boring.

Under her closed eyelids she became aware that the light had altered. Without opening her eyes she absorbed that fact and with it the realisation that she had been asleep. It was a soft, warm dusk now. Blue shadows thickened in the room. A sound behind her made her start and she opened her eyes, jumping. It was only as she sat up on the bed that she realised that she had been woken up by someone tapping on the window. They were tapping there now, their face pressed against the glass, nose flattened, eyes magnified.

Still dopey with sleep, Deborah struggled up, backing away from the window.

The tapping came slightly louder but still muffled, as though done with wary caution.

"Oh, my God!" Deborah groaned, suddenly recognising that face, odd though it looked when it was squashed against glass.

I should have known, she thought, marching towards the window. She yanked it up and the face fell forward with a squawk of protest.

"Hey, watch it! You nearly decapitated me!"

"Don't tempt me." She looked at him, yearning to bring the window down on his extended neck. "What are you doing here?"

"Give me a hand. Tyrell is prowling around the garden, and I want to get in before he spots me."

"I've a good mind to shout for him," Deborah threatened without seriously meaning it.

"Get out of the way and let me climb through." Rodney grasped the sill and heaved his thin body over it, straightening to give her a grin.

"How did you find us?" she asked.

"I spotted someone I knew driving back to Venice. We had a chat and he told me where you were."

"He?" Deborah stared.

"He's a photographer, freelance. His girl apparently has a passion for Tyrell. She was in the car, breathing fire and vengeance all over the place."

"Teresa Scalatio!" Deborah moaned.

"Oh, is that who she was? Now she's what I call sexy." Rodney had a familiar gleam in his eye. "I fancied her." He looked Deborah over, taking in her dishevelled condition without pleasure. "No offence, but Tyrell made the wrong choice, if you ask me."

"I didn't ask you." Deborah felt bitter as she stared at his cynical smile. "What are you doing here?"

"Oh, come off it. I don't have to tell you that. Hal wants your side of the story—exclusive. What's the point of having one of our own people in the middle of a big news story if we don't get anything out of it?"

"I suppose it would be naïve of me to ask if any of you felt any sort of loyalty to me as a friend and colleague?"

Rodney had begun to wander around, inspecting the room. She could see that he was mentally recording it for use in his story later. He looked over his shoulder, his eyes pitying and amused.

"What I've always liked about you, Deb, was your sense of humour."

"I haven't got one," she agreed furiously. "And stop doing an inventory, because if you write one line about this I'll kill you, I swear I will!"

He paused beside the bed, measuring it with his eye. "A bit small. Or has Tyrell got the double bed elsewhere?"

Deborah hit him. He was taken off guard and fell across the room, swearing and catching his leg on the corner of the bed. Deborah froze, staring at the door. Rodney had made too much noise. Had Matthew heard it?

CHAPTER EIGHT

RODNEY clambered to his feet, rubbing the back of his head. "What did you do that for? It was a fair question. Anyone would think I'd insulted you!"

"You did," Deborah hissed. "And keep your voice down! Do you want him to hear?"

Lowering his voice, Rodney said: "I don't see what's insulting about noticing that that's a single bed."

"It's a single bed because I shall be sleeping in it alone."

He laughed rudely. "Do you expect me to believe that after seeing those photos of the two of you?"

"Drop dead," Deborah told him, going to the door and listening for sounds of movement outside.

"I just find it unbelievable," Rodney murmured.

"What?" She turned and he was staring at her fixedly, his eyes running over her from head to foot.

"That you should have caught a guy like that," Rodney told her with brutal honesty. "I mean, you're not bad-looking, of course," he added hurriedly, seeing the look in her eye. "In fact, I've always fancied you myself, but you certainly aren't so spectacular that I'd have expected someone like Tyrell to flip his lid over you. He's very eligible and he's got all that money. I can see why you would want him, but Tyrell must have had a pretty wide choice. What made him pick you?''

"I tripped him up.'' Deborah would have liked to hit him again, but she contented herself with merely looking at him with intense dislike.

Rodney saw the expression and moved away carefully. "Hal sends his congratulations, by the way. He said he hopes you won't forget your poverty-stricken old friends now you're going to be a millionaire's wife.''

"Oh, I won't forget them,'' Deborah promised with vicious softness. "If I ever set eyes on Hal again I'll impale him on his own spike!''

"How did you come to meet Tyrell, anyway?''

Deborah was still listening for indications of Matthew's presence near her room and getting none. She glanced over her shoulder. "We ran into each other. Mind your own business.''

"Have a heart, Deb! I've got to get some sort of story or Hal will eat me alive.''

"I'll lend him a knife and fork,'' she assured him.

"Don't be like that. When's the wedding?''

"Rodney, there's the window. Get back out of it and vamoose!''

"You're angry because I said you weren't in the beauty queen class,'' Rodney mused. "Funny thing about women—you can say anything you like to them except hint they aren't Helen of Troy and Brigitte Bardot rolled into one. If you so much as breathe a word of criticism about their looks you get your eyes scratched out.''

"Rodney, you're putting ideas into my head,'' Deborah said very sweetly. "If you don't get out of here that's just what I will do!''

Rodney sat down on her bed. "You're facing a lot of competition, you know. Tyrell's life is littered with lovely ladies."

Deborah felt a little dart of anger. She recognised the style of phrasing. That was Rodney in full flow. She could see the sort of angle he was going to use when he did the story. Matthew's past was going to be paraded to the hilt.

"Get out!" she bit out, advancing on him.

"His last lady love is screaming her head off in London," Rodney told her. "Now she's a real beauty. I wouldn't mind her."

Deborah grabbed his shoulder and tried to haul him up. Laughing, he caught her by the waist and pulled her down towards him. "What's the matter, Deb? Jealous?"

"Why, you..." Pummelling him angrily, she tried to free herself, but was pulled down on the bed. "Let me go!" Deborah gasped breathlessly as she found herself on her back with Rodney laughing down at her; a distinct glint in his eyes.

Deborah lay still, glaring back at him. "If you do—" she began, seeing that he was about to kiss her, but her sentence was never ended. There was a movement behind her and Rodney looked up, his mouth dropping open. Before he could say a word he was dragged away, spluttering, and marched to the window.

"Now look," he managed to stammer, "you can't..."

Matthew tipped him out of the window without waiting to hear the end of that sentence. Deborah heard Rodney land and winced. Matthew slammed down the window and swung, his face black with temper.

"I presume that that little ferret was the hero who's been making you sob into your pillow lately? Your taste is suspect, Miss Linton. I'd expected someone a little more exciting."

Taken aback, she opened her mouth to put him right, but he didn't wait for confirmation of his guesswork, going on with his angry remarks, riding over her first stammered denial.

"I hope you didn't tell him anything you're likely to regret, because if you did I shall make you very sorry. When I heard voices in here I wondered if you'd developed talent as a ventriloquist, but just in case I came round the house to have a check through the window. Lucky I did. If you've denied our engagement you'll look very silly when you have to un-deny it. Was he in your little plot to nail me for *Probe*?"

"I told you, there was no plot. You know Teresa set that photographer on our tails."

"Oh, yes, but you decided to take advantage of that, didn't you? You and *Probe* have wanted to get me ever since that business four years ago. You want to use the old smear tactic on me. Well, you aren't going to get the chance. If I see any more *Probe* ferrets around here I'll wring their necks!" He turned and glanced out of the window. "Your boy-friend is making off like a bat out of hell. I think he got the message."

"He's not my boy-friend. He just works with me."

"I saw that," said Matthew on a grating note. He swung and looked at her with distaste. "No wonder newspaper stories are so badly written if that's the way you all behave! Rolling about on the bed laughing and kissing each other. Do you think I'm stupid? The man's your lover!''

Deborah's face was burning, with rage rather than embarrassment. "Oh, think what you like!"

"I don't need your permission to do that."

"No, you just need a brain operation."

"That's it, descend to childish insult when you can't think of anything to say!"

"I'll descend to kicking your teeth in if you talk to me like that again!"

"Lady, you are beginning to annoy me," said Matthew on a deep, harsh note, moving towards her.

Deborah felt all her nerves leap in alarm. "Don't you touch me," she said, backing.

"I was beginning to believe all your wide-eyed stuff about love being too serious to play around with," Matthew told her through his teeth. "I must have been insane to believe a word a woman said to me, let alone a word a journalist said. You'll never pull the wool over my eyes again. If you can roll around on a bed with a little snake like that you can do it with me!"

That temper of his had shot through the top of his head. She could almost see flames coming through his black hair, and his blue eyes were glittering with rage.

"If there's one thing I can't stand it's being made a fool of," he told her as he caught hold of her arms.

Struggling angrily, she was pulled down on to the bed. She forgot what she had learnt about waiting for his temper to cool—her own temper was too high for her to remember anything. She kicked and wriggled, her body trapped under the weight of his, her head jerked round by his hand until he could find her mouth. The bruising force of that kiss silenced and stifled her. She had her hands against his chest now, but she wasn't hitting him any more. She involuntarily curled her fingers into her shirt and Matthew's angry kiss softened as he felt her giving way.

His fingers caressed her gently and Deborah was horrified to hear herself groaning, to feel her body dissolving in a honeyed flood of pleasure at the stroking movements which ran from her breast to her thigh.

Her hands crept round to his back and held him closer, one of them running up into his hair, touching his powerful nape with delicate little brushes of her fingertips.

For the first time she didn't want him to stop. Her body was arching with an involuntary invitation and Matthew's thigh parted her own, his kiss deepening in pressure and excitement.

Afterwards she wondered if she would have let him take her, but fortunately the sexual climate was abruptly destroyed by the flash of a camera outside the window.

"Oh, hell!" Matthew broke out, rearing with fury.

He was at the window, a few seconds later. Deborah lay, trembling, shivering, a hand over her face.

She heard Matthew fling up the window and climb out. She heard him running, shouting. There was a crash and a string of irate swear words. Deborah did not go to the window to see what had happened; she could gather only too clearly. Matthew had tripped over one of the exposed roots which marred the dry soil.

Getting off the bed, she stumbled to the washbasin. She ran the tap until the water was ice-cold and then splashed her hot face for a moment. From outside she heard a car engine start, and a short time later Matthew came back through the window.

"There is a door, you know," Deborah said wearily through the folds of the towel with which she was drying her face.

"No doubt you'll be gratified to hear that your lover got away with his picture."

"He's not my lover!"

"I know what I saw when I watched you through the window. You were having a good laugh at my expense, I've no doubt." As Matthew talked his voice hardened. "What sort of a swine is he, anyway, taking pictures of his girl with another man?"

"I'm not his girl." Deborah hung up the towel neatly, adjusting it as though intent on nothing else. "The truth is . . ."

"Truth? That's a funny word for you to use."

Bristling, she snapped: "Stop using that tone to me!"

The blue eyes raked her, making her stiffen. "Just remember—if I catch him with you again I'll flatten him, so unless you want him in a permanently mangled condition, don't let him back into this house."

Deborah drew a long breath, counting to ten. Matthew was in one of his tempers again. She remembered that it was wisest to let him cool down. Politely she said: "Your clothes need brushing—they're covered with dust from where you fell over that root."

His reply was incoherent, but she got the message. When he had slammed the door she bolted it, then closed the window and drew the curtains. If Rodney came back he could tap until his knuckles bled, she wouldn't let him in again.

His remarks about Matthew's past had somehow embedded themselves inside her and now they were stinging like poisoned thorns. She had forgotten for a moment, while he was making love to her, that Matthew Tyrell was an expert at raising a woman's temperature. Those coaxing, inciting hands had made her forget all common sense for a while and she was furious with herself for being such a fool.

If she was writing the story herself she knew how she would have automatically described Matthew Tyrell. International playboy, jet-set leader, tycoon, nightclub darling—the instinct to reach for a cliché shortcut to describe someone like him was nailed into her head. It saved time, Hal would say. People aren't reading our paper for highflown prose, darling, he would tell her. They want the facts as succinctly as they can get them. A short cut saves time and energy. However long you spend polishing your phrases, they'll forget them by tomorrow morning. Just give them the story in as readable a fashion as you can and forget writing like Henry James. She could remember her first attempt at a news story as if it had happened yesterday. Hal had read it, said: "Clever little darling, aren't we?" Then he had screwed the sheet into a ball, chucked it at his wastepaper basket and watched it roll away into a corner. "Now go and write me a crisp paragraph giving me the facts—the facts, nothing but the facts."

Deflated, she had done just that, and although from time to time she had been tempted into another effort at deathless prose, by and large she had remembered to write the way Hal wanted her to write. News had a brief life. Newspapers were dead within twenty-four hours.

Rushing from one story to another, one learnt how to get the point home, however many clichés one had to use to save time.

Matthew Tyrell's love life would come out in print as one long string of clichés, of course. He was a gift to a gossip columnist. *Probe* had not spared his private life when they were investigating him. Deborah hadn't had anything to do with that side of the story but she remembered it vaguely. His name had been coupled with that of a succession of beautiful girls, from film stars to pop singers.

He certainly had a formidable technique, she thought angrily. She could kick herself for having responded to it. She was beginning to suspect that Matthew Tyrell was habit-forming. The more he kissed her the more she found herself enjoying it—and that was dangerous.

He would probably never have got anywhere with her if they had not met while she was in emotional turmoil over another man. She hadn't let herself be talked into bed in the past because she was never sufficiently tempted by anyone who tried. It is so easy to be self-controlled when you are not tempted in the first place. Deborah had never met a man with Matthew's array of weapons before. Her usual freezing manner did not seem to operate with him. They had got to know each other too well, too quickly. She was beginning to be seriously worried by him.

Her strong views about casual sex hadn't been enough to stop Matthew Tyrell from getting to her. She despised herself for giving way with such abandon after all she had said to him. She had to be out of her mind. Matthew Tyrell might fancy her as one of his playmates for a while, but that was all. There was nothing more to his lovemaking than self-indulgent impulse. If she had given way all along the line she would be hating herself a lot more by now.

Crimson flooded into her face as she suddenly remembered Rodney and the photo he had snatched just now. He would be on his way with it, laughing like mad.

Any doubt in Rodney's mind about her relationship with Matthew would have disappeared after seeing that passionate kiss.

The sound of a car engine suddenly interrupted her thoughts. She stood, listening, heard the engine stop and unbolted her door. Matthew was nowhere in sight. Deborah ran through the hall and out on to the terrace. The black shape of the car stood some way off and in the headlights she saw Matthew moving about beside it.

Deborah tore towards it, recognising it as the car which had brought them. The driver got back into it and the engine started again.

"Stop!" Deborah shouted, waving both arms.

Matthew dropped the cases he was carrying and leapt into her path, pinioning her to his chest.

"Let me go! I'm going back with him!"

"No, you're not. You're staying here with me!"

Eye to eye, they glared at each other. Deborah felt like biting him. "I'm not staying here all night with you!"

"That's just what you are doing," Matthew said, and she felt her pulses leap at the look in his blue eyes.

The car drove away. Over his shoulder Deborah watched it despairingly. Her last chance of escape from this dangerous man was vanishing right in front of her eyes.

"You can't keep me here against my will!"

"Just watch me."

"If Teresa knows we're here, the *paparazzi* will be swarming all over the place soon," she pointed out.

Matthew smiled. "No, they won't. I've taken care of that."

Her heart sank. "I swear I've no intention of writing a word about you." He just smiled. Infuriated, she broke out: "In fact, I never even want to hear your name again!"

"Charming," he said, angry blue eyes flashing at her. "You certainly have a way with words. You don't need a stiletto up your sleeve. You have far deadlier weapons, don't you?"

He released her and walked away, carrying their cases. Deborah stiffly followed him into the villa and watched a moth fluttering around the light. Matthew went out, came back with a large cardboard box.

"Food," he told her. "I told him to bring steak. I'm hungry."

"I'm your guest, very much against my will," Deborah spat back. "You can do the cooking this time."

"You'll regret it," Matthew sighed. "I'm the world's worst cook, I'm afraid."

"I'll grin and bear it," said Deborah, shrugging. "Call me when the meal is ready."

As she walked out he said tersely: "Your case."

"Would you bring it to my room, please? Guests don't carry their own cases."

After a little silence he came after her with the case and dropped it on the floor. Turning, he gave her a hard stare. "Keep this up and I may lose my temper with you."

"I'm getting used to your temper. I've rarely seen you without it."

"That's a lie. I'm generally very even-tempered. I only lose it when I'm provoked."

"If that's what you want to believe, don't let me stop you, but I would say you were a man who lived on the edge of a volcano."

Matthew flexed his hands at his side as though longing to put them round her throat. "You're a very annoying female. Years of living alone and doing a man's job, I suppose."

"That is rank chauvinism. You do a man's job and your temper is much worse than mine."

"I've never met anyone who made me lose it so often." Matthew looked her up and down derisively. "You look like someone who's been up all night. While I'm cooking the worst meal you'll ever have eaten I suggest you make yourself look rather more feminine."

"Get out!" snapped Deborah, so enraged she could scarcely speak at all.

Smiling with satisfaction at having made her face burn, Matthew went.

How he dared call her provoking Deborah could not imagine. In the short time of their acquaintance Matthew Tyrell had annoyed her more often than anyone she could remember. At times she almost got the feeling he was doing it deliberately. He had a quite wicked glint in his eye as he teased her, as though it gave him a lot of fun to see her hackles rise and her face flush with impatience.

A man with a temper like his should be more wary of making other people angry. Anger breeds anger, it flashed between them like sparks from a sudden fire, spreading the conflagration far and wide.

Glancing at herself in the mirror, Deborah groaned. He was right, though; she was not a pretty sight. Bolting the door, she set to work to remedy that. By the time Matthew yelled for her she was ready and sauntered out with the satisfaction of knowing she looked very different.

He was standing in the kitchen, very flushed, his black hair on end like a porcupine's quills, and he didn't look at her as he broke out furiously: "I did warn you, don't say I didn't. If you can eat it, you're welcome. I'd rather eat bread and cheese."

A smell of burning lingered on the air. Deborah regarded the burnt offering on the table.

"I see what you mean." She walked past him to look more closely. "Was it steak?"

Matthew didn't answer. She turned, very casually, and found him inspecting her from head to toe in a leisured way, his brows hovering above the blue eyes with silent comment.

He raised his eyes and looked into hers. He didn't say a word, just whistled softly.

"Thank you," Deborah said gravely.

"My pleasure, I assure you," he murmured, mouth twitching at the corners. "The food may be uneatable, but the scenery will be well worth looking at."

She gave the blackened steak another glance. "I've never been fond of charcoal. What happened to it?"

"I did," Matthew shrugged. "I put it on and then I

decided to fry some onions with it, but while I was peeling and chopping them the steak burnt.''

"For heaven's sake, you must have noticed that smell!''

"Of course I would have done, but I hate the smell of onions, so I chopped them out on the verandah in the open air. It wasn't until I came back in here that I discovered what was happening to the steak. I thought it took longer to cook than that.''

She watched some moths fluttering around the lamp, their powdery wings brushing the ceiling. "You left the door open, didn't you? The place is full of moths!''

"All right, I'm sorry, but I'm not a housewife or a cook!''

"You did it deliberately,'' Deborah accused. "You were making a point.''

He looked innocently at her. "What are you talking about?''

"Oh, get out while I cook us something we can eat,'' she muttered, taking the incinerated steak and chucking it into the bin. Matthew discreetly slid out.

Presumably he never had to cook for himself. He must have people to do that sort of thing for him. Nice for him, Deborah thought blackly. He hadn't exerted himself to make sure the meal was well cooked, though. He had half intended it to be a disaster. She already had a shrewd idea of his capabilities. Matthew Tyrell could do anything he turned his hand to, if he chose—he just hadn't chosen to be a good cook. No doubt he saw domestic tasks as falling within a woman's role. She remembered the way he kept emphasising femininity, complaining about her on that score whenever the occasion arose. Old-fashioned chauvinism, Deborah decided, finding an all-enveloping apron hanging inside one of the cupboards. She hadn't spent all that time making herself look her best just to ruin it by slaving over a hot stove. Tying it round her waist, she set to work.

Matthew had ruined two perfectly good pieces of steak, but the man who brought their suitcases had also brought a large box of food supplies. Deborah found some more steak in the capacious fridge and began to cook it.

Matthew emerged ten minutes later with a bottle of wine. He sniffed as he poured wine into two glasses. "I love fried onions."

"Good," said Deborah. "I hate them."

He looked at her through his lashes, his mouth curved in wicked amusement. "Do I detect a hint there?"

She was serving the food and didn't answer. Matthew looked at his plate. It was heaped with fried onions. "It looks marvellous. Where did you find the mushrooms?"

"The deep freeze. I took them out at lunch time and they've thawed very nicely." She sat down.

"I'd prefer you without the pinny," Matthew informed her, undoing it at the back.

She took it off and Matthew smiled at her, the warm line of his mouth entirely friendly. "Did I tell you that you looked fantastic?"

Her colour rose. "I think I got a compliment of some sort." A whistle counted as a compliment, she thought, especially accompanied by that look in the blue eyes.

He sat down opposite her and lifted his glass. "Good

food, good wine, good company—what more could a man ask?"

Deborah surveyed him derisively. "What indeed?"

He laughed and began to eat. "I'm beginning to think I shall be bored out of my skull when I say goodbye to you. You certainly make life lively! I can't imagine why you haven't been snapped up before. The men in your life must be as blind as bats."

"You're very kind," she murmured.

"Tell me about your family. Have you any brothers or sisters?"

"A sister," she admitted, beginning to tell him about Andrea. Matthew probed with questions whenever she fell silent, and it wasn't for some time that she realised how much she was telling him about her life. She stopped speaking and sipped some more wine.

"Your father is still sailing between Stockholm and London?"

She nodded. "He loves his job. He wouldn't know what to do with himself if he was stranded on dry land."

"He didn't do a very good job with his family, though," Matthew said quietly. "I can understand his problem, left with two young daughters, but he did rather duck out of responsibility."

"He hadn't a clue how to cope with us," Deborah admitted. "Maybe he should never have married in the first place."

"You don't see much of him?"

"Very rarely," she shrugged. "At Christmas he sometimes turns up at Andrea's to spend a few days with us."

"You spend Christmas with her?"

"Usually."

"You're very close?"

"I suppose so. Andrea tends to see me as a difficult teenager even now. She's a born mother, rather bossy and managing, but she's all the family I've got."

"You're lucky," he said drily. "I've got a family, a big one, the tentacles spread halfway across the world, and they refuse to let you go. I often wish I could call my life my own."

"Are they older or younger than you?"

"I've got two older sisters and one younger one. They're all married and all have children. I've got a younger brother, too. He's married now, and his wife is expecting a baby around Christmas. Apart from that, I've got aunts, uncles, cousins, by the score. The ones who live in England are the worst. They keep tabs on me all the time. I spend my life hiding from them."

Deborah gazed at him, her green eyes wide and thoughtful. "You don't look like a man who comes from that sort of background," she commented.

"What do I look like?" He leaned over the table with a pleased expression, his chin on his hands, like a child who loves to be the centre of attention, delighted to hear himself talked about. Deborah drew back, faintly wary.

"I hadn't thought about it."

"Think now," he urged, smiling.

Deborah felt a frisson of alarm. She had not intended to get herself into a position of intimacy with him, but somehow over the meal they had moved even closer, and she was worried by the way he was looking at her. Matthew Tyrell was adroit with people—she was realising that more and more. He was a born manipulator, gently teasing and nudging people into doing what he wanted. All that charm had its effect, despite her attempts at ignoring it.

"I don't really know you well enough," she said evasively.

Matthew's eyes mocked her. "Coward! Now you really are deceptive. That lovely blonde hair and those big green eyes give no indication of the brain behind them. While a man is busy admiring your figure you're quite capable of cutting his throat before he notices what you're up to."

"And serve him right," said Deborah, trying not to laugh.

"You see? You're rather too alarming for a woman."

Deborah did not like that. Her eyes flashed and Matthew, watching her closely, caught the anger in them and looked even more amused.

"What was he like, this Robert of yours?"

She looked taken aback, the question throwing her into confusion. Glancing down, she played with her wine glass stem. "Attractive."

"What made him so special? He was, I take it. Special, I mean. You wouldn't have flipped over him otherwise. I get the strong impression it was the first time you had ever flipped over anyone."

Deborah hesitated before answering. On impulse she was honest. "I think I was ready for that sort of mistake. For years my job has been the only thing that mattered to me, but when I met Robert I was getting tired of travelling around the world. I wanted to fall in love, I suppose."

"So you did," Matthew murmured gently. "And you picked the wrong man. Or did you?"

She looked up, puzzled. "What do you mean?"

He stared into her eyes, his face serious. "What you've told me about this Robert makes me wonder if you didn't instinctively pick the same sort of man as your father—a man who would duck out on you. We tend to repeat patterns which have deeply affected us in childhood. Without realising what you were doing, perhaps you recognised in Robert the same qualities you had learnt to expect of men from your father."

Deborah was too surprised to answer. She shifted her wine glass, her brows knitting in a frown.

"Or am I being too clever?" Matthew asked.

Deborah looked at the cluttered table. "I'd better clear this up and do the washing-up."

"Now that I can do," said Matthew, rising. He made no comment on her refusal to continue the discussion.

CHAPTER NINE

WHEN they had restored the kitchen to some semblance of order they played cards at the table. Deborah had not been able to evict the moths Matthew had allowed to invade the room. They fluttered around the light making little, excited tapping noises. Beyond the wide picture window the wind sighed in the branches of olive trees and the dark sky was restless and cloudy. A moon rose and picked out black outlines among the escarpment of the hills.

"Are you playing or just lost in thought?" Matthew asked, making her jump, and Deborah turned with an apologetic smile.

"Sorry. You were right about the view. The way the hills roll across the horizon is fantastic."

"It looks better by day."

She played a card half absently and he looked at her in dry appraisal. "Your mind is not on this game." He collected up the cards.

"Who won?"

"I did," Matthew said with emphasis. "Not that you noticed. You look tired. Why don't you get off to bed?"

Deborah stood up, yawning. "Sorry. Yes, I am tired. Goodnight."

Trailing to the door, she heard him murmur: "Sweet dreams." She didn't like the way he said it.

Bolting her door, she got ready for bed and sank into it with a sigh of content. Her head hardly touched the pillow before she was soundly asleep.

Tapping woke her, and she stirred, stretching. The room was filled with morning light and Matthew said beyond the door: "Come on, sleeping beauty, do you want some coffee or don't you?"

She slid out of bed and put on her dressing-gown. When she opened the door he ran a comprehensive glance over her, walked past and put down the tray he was carrying. Deborah felt alive and awake this morning. She had slept without stirring all night.

Matthew drew the curtains. He was dressed, his hair brushed, his face freshly shaved. Sunlight fell into the room and brought it to life. Watching Matthew move away from the window, Deborah became suddenly aware of the odd familiarity she felt towards him. She had a confused moment when she could not even remember how long she had known him. It seemed like years. How many days was it since he came out of the mist when she screamed in that stupid way?

She stared at him, her green eyes wide and slightly dazed. He was pouring a cup of coffee from a large glazed black pot, his body bent, his black hair falling forward to hide the sharp angle of his cheekbone. She watched him idly push it back. "There's still some cream left," he said. "Do you want some in your coffee?"

She hardly heard him.

He looked up and their eyes met. Deborah flushed. "Cream?" he asked again, beginning to smile.

"Thank you."

I've got to get away from him, Deborah thought. What's the matter with me? She had to be imagining this peculiar feeling inside her chest. Accepting the cup, she sipped it to cover her embarrassment and Matthew walked to the door.

"I've had my breakfast. I let you sleep."

"That was thoughtful. Thank you." She couldn't help speaking in a stilted fashion. She was horribly self-conscious and she couldn't meet his eyes.

"I'm glad you're beginning to see my good points," he said with a mocking inflection before going out.

Is that what I'm doing? she thought, staring across the room at the pale blue sky. Or am I on the rebound from Robert, ricocheting like a lost tennis ball? Ever since she met Matthew she had been in an emotional dither. It was very unlike her. She had never thought of herself as an emotional person. She had learnt to run her life with efficiency and calm. Robert had knocked her off balance for a while and, coming to Venice, she had walked straight into Matthew. Ever since she had been kept off balance, unable to think clearly.

That's what I've got to do! Think. She went over to bolt the door. Finishing her coffee, she drew the curtains again before taking a quick shower and dressing. She put on a pair of white jeans and a dark blue cotton T-shirt. They made her look cool and sensible again, and she eyed herself reprovingly. Pull yourself together, you stupid fool, she told her reflection. You're beginning to let him get to you, and that would be a recipe for a total disaster. Matthew Tyrell had no place in his life for someone like her, except one she had no intention of filling. He was strictly on the banned list.

"And don't you forget it," she murmured as she carried the tray of coffee out to the kitchen.

"That's the first sign," Matthew informed her, looking up from the book he was reading.

"What is?"

"Talking to yourself."

"First sign of what?" As he opened his mouth with that wicked smile in his eyes she said hastily, "No, don't tell me. I'd rather not know."

"I'm sure you wouldn't," he replied cryptically.

"Can we go back to Venice today?"

"No." He made no attempt to expand on that. "I thought we could take a walk in the hills, actually. The views can be breathtaking."

Deborah looked up at the rolling landscape beyond the window. It would keep them occupied safely for a few hours. "Why not?" He had said they would stay here for a couple of days. One more day wouldn't hurt her. Tomorrow she was definitely going back to Venice.

"I can hear you thinking," said Matthew, watching her.

Startled, she looked at him. "Oh? What am I thinking?"

"I should say plotting," Matthew altered. "You get a secretive, conspiratorial look. It won't do you any good. You're staying here until I say you can leave."

"I've got a job waiting for me," she pointed out.

"You're on holiday at the moment."

"So have you got work to do. Won't they be screaming for you back in London?"

"There are plenty of people to keep the wheels turning," he shrugged. "If I'm urgently needed they know where to find me."

"My sister doesn't know where to find me. She'll be very worried if she's been reading the papers."

He considered her. "Send her a telegram. I'll see it gets to her."

Deborah grimaced. "I could hardly explain this set-up in a telegram."

"I thought journalists were good at the pithy phrase."

"I could think of one or two to describe you," she agreed.

"I said pithy, not insulting."

"In your case it would come to the same thing."

Matthew gave her a long stare. "You're a sharp-tongued little scold, has anyone ever told you that?"

"One or two," she admitted.

"And all men?" Matthew suggested.

"I can't remember."

He laughed shortly. "I'm certain of it. I'm beginning to see that there's only one way of dealing with a woman like you." He moved before she had notice of his intentions, and that was something she was beginning to know about him. You had to be very quick to see him coming.

She hadn't been quick enough. Matthew kissed her hard before releasing her. Although the kiss was brief it sent the blood singing through her veins and her face into disturbed confusion. What made her angriest was the fact that she had enjoyed it. To cover the weakness of her own reaction she said coldly: "I do wish you wouldn't do that—it's very boring being grabbed all the time."

Dark colour came into his face, and he gave her a fierce, hard stare before turning away. Deborah was surprised. Those blue eyes had been really angry. She had not expected to get that sort of reaction. She must have flicked his ego, she imagined. No doubt he thought his kisses were always fatal to a woman's heart.

Over his shoulder he said: "I could get to dislike you intensely, Miss Linton."

Deborah almost snapped back, but thought better of it. She did not want him roaring into one of his black tempers again. Anything could happen when Matthew Tyrell hit the roof.

It was as they were resting on top of a steep scrub-strewn hill two hours later that Matthew finally began to unbend. During their slow climb through the olive groves he had been almost totally silent and she had begun to think he was going to be sulking for the rest of the day.

Now, though, he lay back, breathing carefully after the climb, and said with amusement: "You really are out of condition, aren't you?"

"I don't go climbing in the Dolomites often," Deborah agreed.

"What do you do? When you can tear yourself away from your job?"

"Theatre, concerts, the odd party." That reminded her of Robert and she stared at the sky fixedly for a moment until she realised that the sharp pang which had been with her for so many days had not in fact pierced her at the memory of Robert after all. She contemplated that with a mixture of relief and surprise.

Matthew asked her casually about the sort of music she liked. They talked without looking at each other, their heads in shade, their bodies relaxed on the stony hillside.

Matthew told her a funny story about a concert he had been to—the conductor's baton had been so violently waved to and fro that it had suddenly flown from his grasp and hit one of the violinists on the nose. "It brought the whole orchestra to a dead stop for a couple of beats, then they picked up as though nothing had happened."

Deborah began to laugh, imagining the scene, and he rolled over to look down at her, laughing with her.

The laughter went abruptly and his head swooped down. Out here on the quiet hillside with some goats grazing far below them and a handful of noisy black crows on the wing to a feeding ground in the valley, it didn't seem to matter whether she resisted him or not. A kiss was part of the morning. Deborah pushed thought aside and ran her arms around his neck, kissing him back.

Matthew murmured something inaudible against her lips. She felt his arms slide under her, lifting her closer, one of his hands moving in her tumbled blonde hair as he deepened the kiss. Their bodies pressed together without urgency, the warm sensuous movement of his mouth coaxing her into unguarded response.

He lifted his head. Deborah half opened her eyes, feeling drowsy and happy.

Matthew smiled, and she caught the smile a second

before his mouth hit hers again. She recognised the triumph; she had seen it in his face before.

Matthew Tyrell was a man who did not like failing. Her remark about being bored by his earlier kiss had stung him. He had been determined to make her eat her words; he thought he just had.

The drowsiness had gone. So had the lightheaded feeling of happiness. Matthew was kissing her heatedly and now there was an urgency in the way he touched her, held her. Deborah lay in his arms without struggling or responding. Her mind was working at top speed. She had not seriously recognised the danger until now. Matthew had made her wake up to it. While his mouth moved demandingly aginst hers Deborah was facing one really alarming fact.

However casually they had been flung together, however idly Matthew had been making the occasional pass at her, his pursuit had become determined now. He wasn't angry, as he had been in the past when he made love to her like this. The emotion driving him came from a very different source.

She could hear his heart racing. His breathing was rough and quick. The hands moving over her had a dangerous effect on her, and she found her own breath stopping at the insistent intimacy of his caresses.

Matthew had become aware of her lifeless submission. He lifted his head again, desire flickering in his eyes. "Don't fight me, Deborah. Stop running and give in."

She had no chance to respond to that. He was kissing her again almost as he said the last word. Deborah abandoned thought and let herself sweep away on the tide of passion running so high in both of them.

A few moments later Matthew rolled away, taking long, deep draughts of air into his lungs. Deborah lay on her back, staring at the sky as it wheeled overhead.

During those moments the feeling between them had escalated to a height she had not expected. Her response had been the final trigger. Matthew's passion had flared almost into violence as she began to kiss him back. Deborah was perfectly well aware that if they had been alone in the villa it would not have stopped at kissing. There had been a fierce urgency growing inside Matthew and it had been matched by her own needs.

"We'd better start back." Matthew sat up, running a hand through his dishevelled hair.

She could not look at him. Her face was hot and disturbed. Getting up slowly, angrily conscious of shaking like a leaf, she began to move down the hill.

Matthew was almost as silent on the way down as he had been on the way up, but from time to time she felt him glancing at her, and she was further disturbed by the look in his eyes.

He really thought he had her. His blue eyes held a smile Deborah disliked. She thought ahead to the villa, the night time when they would be quite alone in that dangerous intimacy, and her panic grew with every step.

When Matthew forced her to accompany him to the villa he had had just this in mind. She was certain of that now. He had been angry with her and determined to stop *Probe* publishing any more damaging stories about him, but he was a man who liked women. He had made it clear from the start that he found her attractive.

He had been moving in on her for days and now he had demolished all her resistance.

Deborah began to get both angry and frightened. She was not joining the long list of conquests Matthew Tyrell had made. She had no wish to see herself in that sort of category or to read newspaper gossip about herself.

She had to get away from him. But how?

As they came in sight of the villa they saw the cars. Matthew stopped dead, swearing under his breath.

"I knew they'd catch up with us sooner or later," Deborah said with angry satisfaction. She knew her own tribe. They never gave up on a living story, although they would drop a dead one without a second's hesitation. Nothing was too much trouble for them if they decided it was worthwhile. They would have crawled here on their hands and knees if they had had no other way of getting here.

Matthew would have backed out of the way if he had not been spotted by the roving eye of one reporter. A moment later they were surrounded and under siege again. Deborah was past caring. She was far more worried about Matthew Tyrell now. She almost felt like kissing the *paparazzi* as they exploded into questions and snatched photos.

Rodney was among them. While Matthew was curtly refusing to answer something one of the others had asked, Deborah caught Rodney's eye, and he gave her a resentful look. She edged slightly away from Matthew and secretly touch Rodney's hand. He looked surprised and wary.

Silently Deborah mouthed: "Back of the villa."

Rodney watched her lips moving. His brows lifted.

"Wait for me," Deborah mouthed.

One of the others had seen the silent exchange and was trying to catch what was being said. Deborah turned away and waited while Matthew answered a few more questions. He put an arm round her waist and they fought their way through the milling crowd into the villa.

"Where are those men?" Matthew burst out as the door opened and shut.

"Men?" Deborah stared at him, bewildered.

"I paid for protection," Matthew said fiercely, "and I'm not getting it. There should have been men on the gate keeping those bastards at arm's length."

"So that's how you meant to do it," Deborah exclaimed, light dawning. "I wondered why we hadn't seen them around."

"I don't leave anything to chance," said Matthew.

They heard shouting outside. Matthew advanced on the window and exclaimed, "Ah, at last!"

Deborah stood at his shoulder and watched as a small group of very large, muscular men drove the *paparazzi* out like sheepdogs herding sheep.

"I'll have a few words with them about this," grated Matthew, going out of the front door.

The moment he had gone Deborah rushed into her own room. She flung her clothes back into the suitcase, gathered all her things together and opened the window.

Rodney rose from a ragged clump of thorn bushes, glancing past her at the villa in a nervous way. "Sure Tyrell's not about? My shoulder still aches from the way he threw me out of the window last time."

Deborah did not waste any sympathy on him. She had almost enjoyed the way Matthew dealt with him. Handing out her case, she asked: "Where's your car?"

Rodney automatically accepted the case, staring at her in surprise. "What's going on?"

"Never mind that. Where's your car?" She climbed out of the window while he watched her blankly.

"End of the lane. Deb, what are you up to now? Why the case? Where are you going? Where's Tyrell?"

She crept to the corner of the villa. She could hear Matthew's voice somewhere out at the front, speaking in crisp fierce Italian, and a low murmur from another man in reply.

"I'm coming with you," she told Rodney in a low voice. "Run, and whatever you do, keep well down. Matthew mustn't see us. We have got to get away before he realises I've gone."

They had to make their way through the thick, rough brush which skirted the villa. It was not easy terrain; the ground was uneven and stony, thick with thorns. She was very grateful for the protection of her jeans. They crawled along with bent heads until they reached the shelter of the olive grove and could run, dodging from tree to tree.

Deborah constantly expected to hear Matthew shouting behind them. She did not dare to look round, but her nerves prickled with anxiety every inch of the way.

When they reached the low stone wall which bordered the villa grounds Rodney dropped her case over before joining it, giving Deborah a hand to climb the wall too.

His car was a hundred yards away. It wasn't until she was in the car and heard the engine fire that Deborah began to breathe more slowly. She stared at the white outline of the little villa through the trees. Rodney shot away, watching the road in his driving mirror.

"No one is else is coming," he told her with relief. "Okay, what's going on?"

"Mind your own business!"

"Come on," said Rodney, his face impatient. "You're running out on Tyrell. Why? Quarrelled already?"

"I've got nothing to say." She paused and said with bitter irony: "No comment." She had never thought she would seriously be in a situation where she would have to say that. She laughed and said it again: "No comment, so don't ask any more questions."

That was like telling the tide to go back. Rodney boiled over with questions and had no scruples about asking them, however intimate or embarrassing.

When Deborah refused to answer he drifted into talking about other aspects of the story. She discovered that Matthew had had the villa estate carefully guarded over the hours since they arrived. He had had a body of men patrolling the walls of the garden.

"Every time someone made a try to get in they came back in a rush. The men had damned great wolfhounds with them. Several people ended up missing a part of their trousers and limping from nasty bites."

"Good," Deborah muttered. "I wish I could have seen it."

"Have you forgotten whose side you're on?" Rodney eyed her sideways. "Women are so emotional. A sexy swine like Tyrell really knows how to get at women, doesn't he? And I thought you were a professional!"

Deborah ignored that. She stared at the road, feeling sick and tired.

"Where are we going?" Rodney demanded. "Or can't I ask that, either?"

Deborah pulled herself out of the dark thoughts which had been absorbing her. "What?"

"Are we going back to Venice?"

"No," she said, thinking fast. "He would have the airport there covered. Take me to Rome."

"What is going on?" Rodney asked pleadingly. "Come on, Deb, be a pal—give!"

"Just drive," Deborah told him.

"You're being damned selfish!" Rodney erupted.

"Selfish?" She stared at him, dumbfounded.

"I know it's your story, but I thought we were friends."

"What on earth made you think that?" she asked wryly, almost tempted to laugh at his sulky face.

"Well, we've worked together well enough in the past," Rodney said. "If you're on to something big with Tyrell you might let me in on it. You're using my help to get away. Aren't I going to get anything in return?"

"You might get a black eye," said Deborah.

"I knew you were boxing clever. I told Hal. Deb's doing a Trojan horse on him, I said. She'll come out with something really big. I know Deb, I said. Men don't have a chance with her. She's ice from the neck down. Tyrell may have flipped over her, but she hasn't flipped over him."

Deborah's face burnt. So she hadn't flipped over Matthew Tyrell, hadn't she? She remembered the way she had felt when Matthew made love to her on the hillside only a short time ago, and she swallowed. Giving Rodney a frozen stare, she said: "You're too kind. I'm deeply flattered by the compliment."

He grinned. "I knew I was right about what you were up to. I worked it out in a flash."

Ice from the neck down, am I? Deborah thought. Well, thank you, Rodney, I'll remember that. As far as you're concerned that's just what I am.

She looked into the driving mirror. The road behind was still clear, but she knew Matthew Tyrell now and she couldn't relax. When he got back into the villa and discovered that she had gone he would be after them, and he could move at quite a speed.

"Don't slow down until we get to Rome," she told Rodney.

"It's a long drive," he complained. "It would be much quicker if we flew."

"I told you, he'll have the airport watched the minute he realises I've gone."

"What have you been up to?" Rodney burst out, turning his head to stare at her. "What's the story, Deb? You can't keep it to yourself."

"Just drive," Deborah insisted, her eyes on the mirror. "He moves like lightning. If he catches up with us he might just break your neck this time."

Rodney looked like a nervous rabbit, a muscle twitching beside his mouth. The car flashed forward like a bullet from a gun.

"Why my neck?" Rodney asked plaintively. "It strikes me that it's you he's after."

Deborah felt a shiver run down her spine. How right

you are, she thought. She hadn't admitted it to herself until this moment, but now she did. Matthew Tyrell was right behind her and she was shaking with nerves at the prospect of him catching up with her. She told herself he would just shrug when he found she had escaped. Why should he pursue her, anyway? She laced her cold hands in her lap. They were trembling. She knew Matthew would follow them and she knew why. During those moments on the hillside his pursuit had become deadly serious, and she knew enough about his determination to have his own way to know that flight would not put him off. Matthew Tyrell was after her, all right.

CHAPTER TEN

"WHAT do you mean, it was all a mistake?" Andrea stared at her, disbelief and impatience in her face. "Those pictures weren't a mistake." She looked at Kerry, who was driving a large yellow lorry across the floor, making a rumbling noise. Andrea lowered her voice, her eyes full of meaning. "I couldn't believe my own eyes. Deb, how could you?"

Flushed, Deborah shifted her feet. "Nothing happened. Can't you get that through your head? The pictures were sheer accident."

Kerry drove past her feet, one wheel running over her shoe. "Sorry, Auntie Deb," he said absently, driving on without looking up.

"Take that thing outside," Andrea ordered, but her mind wasn't on her children, for once. She went on peeling potatoes and talking to Deborah in a fast, angry voice. "I wouldn't like to repeat some of the things the neighbours said!"

"Then don't," Deborah implored.

"It's all been very embarrassing. I'd never expected you to do such a thing."

"I didn't do anything." Deborah had already told her that over and over again, but she might as well have saved her breath. Andrea believed what she read in newspapers.

"Mind you, he's very attractive, I suppose." Andrea looked at her obliquely with a hopeful gleam in her eye. "What's he like?"

"I don't want to talk about him," Deborah said, a faint shiver sliding down her back like ice water. She could not think of a way of describing Matthew Tyrell adequately. She was still nervously jumping every time someone knocked at her door or every time the phone rang. She had not felt safe until Rodney saw her on to the plane for London. They had reached Rome without being intercepted, but Deborah had half expected to find Matthew at the airport and even now she did not feel easy in her mind.

"Why are you so secretive?" Andrea looked at her fixedly, trying to read her expression. "You never tell me anything."

"I'm telling you something now, but you refuse to believe me. There's nothing between me and Matthew Tyrell. The whole thing has been blown up out of thin air."

"What are those pictures, then?"

"I've explained those," Deborah asserted wearily.

"You don't expect me to believe that fairy story?" Andrea washed her hands at the kitchen sink, talking over her shoulder. "Tom was very shocked, I can tell you."

"I'm sorry Tom was shocked," said Deborah, wanting to scream and break things, "but he needn't be. I'm not Matthew Tyrell's mistress or his fiancée."

"Deborah!" Andrea gave Kerry's bent head a glance. "*Pas devant les enfants.*"

Deborah looked at Kerry. "Brmm, brmm," he went, rolling his lorry under the table. "He isn't listening," Deborah said defensively.

"They're always listening," Andrea observed darkly. "Kerry, take your lorry and play in the garden."

"It's too cold," he said invisible under the table.

"You see? He's listening, all right," Andrea said, fishing under the table for him.

He came out, wriggling, his lorry under his arm. "Outside!" his mother ordered.

"When are you going to be married, Auntie Deb?" Kerry asked, his round eyes lifted to Deborah's flushed face. "Can I come? I want to be a pageboy. When Peter's sister got married, he was a pageboy and he got three pieces of wedding cake. He only ate the icing—he doesn't like cake with raisins in. I do. I like picking out the currants and peel and eating them. I'll get a day off school if I'm a pageboy. Peter got a day off school."

"Out!" repeated Andrea, shoving him through the door with unloving determination. "And don't come back until I call you."

They heard him driving his lorry down the garden path. "Brmm, brmm, brmm!"

Andrea shut the door. "I told you he was listening. Ears like radar, pick up everything. And the neighbours don't scruple to ask him questions, either. What he doesn't pick up around the house he gets from them."

"People talk too much," said Deborah, watching her sister plug the kettle in and start making tea.

"Some people don't talk enough," Andrea told her. "You, for instance. You didn't tell me you'd walked out on Robert."

Deborah flinched. "That's something else I don't want to discuss."

"Is there anything you do? I'm your sister, in case you'd forgotten."

"How could I forget? You never miss an opportunity to remind me."

Andrea gave her an offended look. "That's very nice! If I didn't worry about you, who would? I don't like knowing that my sister is running around with men like Matthew Tyrell and getting up to God knows what. Robert was a very nice man. I like Robert. He would have made you a very good husband."

"A husband was the last thing Robert wanted to be!" Deborah threw at her furiously, too angry to watch what she was saying.

"Oh," Andrea mouthed. The kettle whistled violently and she turned automatically to make the tea. "Deb, you leave me speechless!"

I wish I did, Deborah thought, as Andrea plunged into feverish speech.

"You mean you and Robert... and now this Tyrell man... goodness knows, I'm not narrow-minded, but I don't know what Tom will say, I really don't." Andrea poured tea and sat down with a bump. "What must Dad be thinking?"

I know what I'm thinking, Deborah thought. I wish I could just get up and walk away from all this, but Andrea would never forgive me. I've got to sit here and listen and try to soothe her down, and I wouldn't mind that so much if she would only believe me, but she won't. I'd have to produce the Angel Gabriel in my defence before she'd even listen to a word.

Families were a mixed blessing. The world would be a much colder, lonelier place without them, but on the other hand they always felt able to comment all too bluntly about what you did with your life. A friend would be more circumspect, but how did you tell a sister who has practically brought you up to shut up and let you lead your own life? To Andrea, Deborah would always be her little sister. She would never be able to see her as a fully grown adult able to do as she pleased. Andrea would always worry and hector her, fret over her, order her around. Deborah could imagine it happening even when they were both in wheelchairs. You can't easily walk out on your own flesh and blood. You have to grin and bear it when they irritate, bore, infuriate you, because for the rest of your life they are always in the same relation to you. It might be maddening, but it was the price you paid for having them at all, and Deborah knew in her heart that if she quarrelled seriously with her sister it would leave a painful hole in her life.

"I just don't understand," Andrea was saying. "Why did he say you were engaged if you weren't?"

"I told you—to spike *Probe*'s guns."

"I don't believe it," Andrea insisted. "It doesn't make sense. A man like that? With all his money?"

And a temper like Mount Vesuvius, Deborah thought. When Matthew blew his lid it was safer to get out of the way, but she didn't bother to explain that to her sister.

"He must have fancied you," Andrea insisted, and Deborah knew she was flushing and couldn't stop it. Andrea regarded her fixedly.

"I knew it!" she said triumphantly.

Deborah ignored that. She did not want to meet her sister's sharp, probing stare because of what she might reveal.

"Robert rang several times," Andrea told her.

Deborah was taken aback at that. "What did he say?"

"Wanted to know what was going on," Andrea told her rather drily. "What do you expect? He seemed as baffled as I was."

No doubt he had been, Deborah thought. He must have been completely taken by surprise by the news. He would wonder what had been going on behind his back, of course, and look back over their own relationship with new eyes. Matthew had deliberately given the impression that they had known each other secretly for some time and, since Robert had imagined he was the only man in her life, he must have been very startled.

That did not displease her. It restored some of her damaged self-respect.

"You should ring him," Andrea told her. "I promised to ask you to ring when I saw you again."

Deborah did not answer that. She wasn't ringing Robert; he was buried in the past for her now. Matthew had done that. He had got her over a painful and difficult episode in her life. However irritating he had been she had to admit that.

Kerry opened the door and Andrea gave him a ferocious glare. "I thought I told you to stay in the garden?"

"There's a big car outside," Kerry said excitedly. "A man got out and he's coming here."

Deborah's heart thudded. She shot out of her chair, her face hot.

"It's him!" She knew it. She had been expecting him some time or other. "I'm not here. You don't know where I am," she told Andrea.

"What are you talking about?" Andrea gazed at her, open-mouthed. "Oh, you mean it's Matthew Tyrell?"

"Of course it is," Deborah said. The door bell gave a

peremptory ring and went on ringing. "Don't let him in!" Deborah wailed.

Andrea stood up stiffly. "Are you frightened of him?" Her face had the belligerance of someone getting ready for battle.

"Terrified," Deborah said breathlessly.

Andrea stared at her, her eyes searching. "Well, I'm not," she said, her chin jutting out.

"Don't let him come in," Deborah begged, backing as though afraid Matthew would burst through the door. The bell went on ringing in sharp bursts.

"Don't worry, I won't," Andrea assured her, marching towards the door.

"You don't know him. He's like a steamroller."

"Well, he won't roll over me," Andrea promised.

Kerry swung on the door handle, his face excited. "He's got a super car. Can I go and look at it? It's red. I bet it can do a ton. Daddy won't drive fast because Mummy doesn't like it. Have you seen my tooth? It fell out when I was eating dinner at school and I think I swallowed it. If I had two teeth missing I could whistle. Can you whistle, Auntie Deb?"

"Yes," said Deborah, not listening.

"Peter can whistle. He's got two teeth missing. What can you whistle, Auntie Deb? Can you whistle a tune? Whistle a tune for me."

Deborah's whole attention had been given to the sound of voices at the front door, but she had to detach herself from them to look at Kerry's serious little face. He was a healthy, thin boy with freckles on his nose and round, bright eyes. Deborah looked at him with amused affection.

"I'm sorry, what did you say? What do you want me to do?"

"Whistle," said Kerry, not surprised to realise that she hadn't been listening. Grown-ups often didn't. He patiently repeated the story about Peter and asked if Deborah could whistle.

She proved it and he kindly informed her that if she had two front teeth missing she could whistle much better. Then he demonstrated his own missing tooth, his mouth open wide.

"Marvellous," Deborah agreed, inspecting it. "How lucky you aren't an elephant. Their teeth are huge."

"Tusks," Kerry said scornfully. "They have teeth too. They don't chew with their tusks, silly."

"Oh, don't they? I didn't know that," Deborah said humbly.

"It says so in my general knowledge book at school. There's a picture of their teeth. We did teeth last term."

She picked him up and put him on her lap. Wriggling, he protested: "Don't squeeze me so tight, Auntie Deb. It makes my tummy hurt."

"I'm sorry." She kissed his freckled nose as the door opened. Andrea walked in backwards, saying: "Now, listen..."

Over her shoulder Deborah met Matthew's blue eyes. Her arms closed round Kerry tightly. He opened his mouth to protest, but didn't say anything as he saw her face.

"You have no right to force your way in here!" Andrea stuttered indignantly.

Deborah put Kerry down and stood up. She had

known that Andrea wouldn't be able to keep him out if he was determined to get into the house.

He stood in the doorway with Andrea dancing between them in a protective fashion and stared back at Deborah in what she could not avoid recognising as a dangerously controlled intensity.

"So I've caught up with you at last," he gritted through his teeth. "You've led me a pretty dance. I don't give a damn about your judo. I'm going to give you the slapping of a lifetime, and if you break my arm afterwards it will have been worth it!"

Andrea looked bemused, glancing from him to Deborah with wide eyes. Kerry listened entranced, staring.

"Come one step near me and you'll regret it!" Deborah promised, getting ready to bolt for the open door into the garden.

"My sister doesn't have to talk to you if she doesn't want to," Andrea chimed in, bristling. "I can call the police, you know. This is my house and nobody has a right to come into it if I tell them to stay out."

Matthew gave her a glance. "I recognise the family resemblance," he told Deborah.

"What's that supposed to mean?" demanded Andrea, quivering with suspicious outrage.

"Don't ask," Deborah advised wearily.

"Much better not," Matthew agreed.

He took a step around Andrea, who at once moved to check him, giving him a head-on glare. "You aren't just dealing with helpless women."

"Now there's a misplaced adjective if ever I heard one," Matthew said drily.

"Very funny," Andrea snapped. "Just get it through

your head—my sister doesn't want to see you. She isn't your sort of female."

"I know what sort she is," Matthew drawled. "Mrs. Pankhurst has a lot to answer for. I'm black and blue after just a few days of your sister, but I've no intention of letting her get away from me all the same."

Andrea opened and shut her mouth like a stranded fish. Deborah's face began to burn as she met Matthew's eyes.

Andrea looked from Matthew to her and back again like someone at Wimbledon, then she briskly advanced on Kerry. "Go and play in the garden when you're told," she told him, thrusting him out of the door and closing it behind him.

Matthew was across the room the moment Andrea was out of his path. Deborah leapt back too late. He had her wrist clamped in one of his hands and was looking at her with mocking menace.

"Got you!"

"Don't you manhandle me!" Deborah snapped, tugging at her imprisoned wrist. "Andrea . . ."

She looked round and her sister had vanished. Matthew laughed softly. "I see your sister is a realist. I hope you're going to be one too, Deborah, because otherwise you're in for a tough life."

"Will you let me go?" Deborah demanded, lifting her free hand to push him away and finding it caught and held before she had a chance to wriggle free. Matthew jerked her forward and she twisted to avoid his searching mouth, hearing him take an angry breath.

"Damn you, stand still!" he said tersely. "Don't make me lose my temper, Deborah, or I won't be responsible for what I do. I've been chasing you across Europe for what seems like years and I'm in no mood for games.''

"Neither am I,'' she retorted. "I told you I'm not a games-player.''

"I know precisely what you are,'' Matthew muttered. He held both her wrists with one hand and with the other jerked up her head and held it while he kissed her fiercely.

"Don't,'' she mumbled under his mouth, and the heated pressure instantly intensified. Matthew kissed her until she had stopped struggling and was kissing him back, her body melting as he pressed his own against it. A languorous warmth flowed through her. Matthew released her hands and drew her even closer. Deborah curved her arms round his neck and submerged like someone drowning, her whole being given over to the intense excitement Matthew had aroused in her.

He finally drew away, his arms still round her, and gave her a restless look, the blue eyes still violent, his face flushed.

"If you thought running out on me like that would get rid of me, you were very wrong. You could run to the end of the earth, Deborah, and I'd still find you.''

"Do I have to spell it out for you? I refuse to have an affair with you.'' She was trembling and her voice was dry because she knew Matthew had the power to undermine her determination. She hoped she sounded more confident than she felt. At this particular moment she was barely able to stand upright on her own two feet because his violent kisses had left her as weak as a kitten.

"Oh, you refuse to, do you?'' He had a wicked glint in his eye now. She stared defiantly back at him.

"Yes.''

"Care to bet on that?" Matthew's voice was bland and his mouth was almost smiling, although she could see that he was keeping it under control.

"I don't want to get any more involved with you than I am already," Deborah snapped.

His hand slid along her spine, emphasising the intimacy of the way he was holding her. "How involved is that?"

"Let me go!" she flared, beginning to struggle again.

He laughed openly, his eyes teasing. "No, Deborah, I won't let you go—not now, not ever. I admit in the beginning I had an affair in mind. All I knew about you in the first twenty-four hours was that you had a figure I liked looking at and big green eyes which flashed like a semaphore. It occurred to me to make the usual sort of approach, of course it did. But within twenty-four hours things were very different. You hit me like an avalanche and I haven't been the same since."

Deborah's heart missed a beat. She couldn't think of a thing to say, her eyes widening.

"You were made for me," Matthew murmured, smiling down into her eyes. "Custom built, darling. I feel grateful to the swine who sent you off to Venice in tears. If it hadn't been for him we might never have met. I might even stretch a point and ask him to the wedding, if only for the chance of knocking him flat."

"Wedding?" Deborah echoed huskily.

"Wedding," he mocked, grinning.

Flustered and disturbed, she said: "Matt, you're going too fast! I don't belong in your world and you don't belong in mine."

"Then we'll make our own," he said, sweeping that

aside as though it meant nothing. "Is that your only doubt, for heaven's sake?"

"I just wouldn't fit."

"You can adapt to anything. Look at the way you wore that mink—to the manner born."

"Oh, Matt..."

"You loved wearing it, admit it."

"There are so many other things," she groaned.

"I'll iron them all out for you."

"Don't be so damned sure of yourself!" Her colour flared into a hectic flush.

"Don't get into one of your tempers," he warned.

"Don't be so high-handed! You can't just take me over and dictate my whole life."

"That's just what I'm going to do," he assured her relentlessly.

She felt him moving closer and said breathlessly, "You haven't thought about this."

"I've thought of nothing else for the last two days."

"Two days isn't long enough."

"It's far too long for me," Matthew muttered grimly.

"A week ago I thought I was in love with another man! Doesn't that tell you anything?" Deborah had a sense of desperation. He was being more than usually obstinate and she did not have a clue what to say to him because her own heart was going so fast she found it difficult to talk at all.

"It tells me you can make mistakes," Matthew informed her casually. "It tells me you're human. It tells me you need me."

"I need time!" she wailed.

"After we're married you'll have all the time you

need," he promised, kissing her neck just below her ear.

"Will you listen to me, Matt?" she demanded, pushing at his chest without any hope of getting him to move back.

"For the rest of my life," he promised softly, his lips moving to her lobe and playing with it.

"You wouldn't want to marry me on the rebound from another man, would you?"

"I don't believe you are on the rebound from another man," Matthew murmured, moving across her cheek to her lips. "I don't believe you really cared twopence for him. It was just a mistake. I think you love me. I don't think you're ready to believe it yet. If you insist, I'll wait until you're as sure as I am, Deborah, but don't try to send me away while you make up your mind because I'm not going."

"You're the most obstinate man I've ever met," Deborah groaned.

"Determined," he substituted smilingly.

"Obstinate I said and obstinate I meant!"

"Darling," he said, brushing her mouth with his lips. She tried not to meet the kiss with response and failed miserably. Matthew gave her a satisfied, amused smile.

"See what I mean?"

"Matt," Deborah began huskily, "can't you see how ridiculous, how absurd it is? I can't be in love with you so soon after thinking I was in love with Robert."

"We've agreed that that was an illusion. You were ready to fall in love with the first man who showed signs of response and I think you instinctively chose a man who would duck out on you. You were conditioned by your childhood into choosing someone as unreliable as your father, but you had enough sense to walk out on him once you realised the sort of man he was.''

She sighed, her brows knitting. "Even so. . .''

"Even so nothing,'' Matthew broke in with a fierce voice. "I'm not missing out on my chance of happiness because you haven't got the nerve to take a risk with me. If I have to handcuff you to my wrist I'll get you to the altar, Deborah, so stop arguing and accept that it's going to happen.''

"Don't you push me around!'' She threw back her head and gave him an infuriated glare, her green eyes sharp.

"I think that's just what you need,'' said Matthew. "You're too headstrong. You need firm handling.''

"Just try it!''

"I intend to,'' he promised, looking amused.

"And don't laugh at me!''

"Don't make me laugh, then,'' Matthew teased.

"I'm trying to make you see sense!''

"That's funny. That's what I'm trying to make you see. One of us has to have her ideas wrong.''

"Oh, of course, it would be me who was wrong. It couldn't by any chance be you?''

He nodded. "Right, it couldn't be me. I'm famous for my common sense.''

"Not to mention your rotten temper!''

"After we're married I hope you'll try to remember not to harp on little things like that,'' he complained, smiling at her in a way that made her heart turn over again.

"Matt—'' she began, and was silenced by a kiss that took her breath away and made her sway weakly forward against him, clinging to his wide shoulders with both hands, her mouth turned up to his possession without any attempt at evasion.

He lifted his head a moment later and gave her a slow, warm smile.

"Convinced? Or do you need some more evidence?"

"I need my head examined," Deborah muttered, leaning her head on his shoulder.

There was a tap at the door and Matthew gave her a conspiratorial grin. "You sister checking that I haven't strangled you?"

Andrea put her head round the door and her face stiffened as she took in the intimacy of their embrace.

"I thought you might like some coffee," she said, with the expression of one wishing to say something very different.

"A good stiff whisky might be more appropriate," Matthew told her. "Proposing to your sister is worse than doing three rounds with a heavyweight!"

Andrea looked sharply at Deborah, her face changing.

"She hasn't said yes," Matthew added with amusement. "On the other hand, every time she says no I shall kiss her until she stops."

"Next time I want to get away from it all I'll avoid Venice like the plague," Deborah said to herself, not bothering to lift her head from Matthew's shoulder.

"Next time you'll be chained to my wrist," Matthew promised.

Andrea said on a dry note: "If you want me I'll be in the kitchen." She went out, closing the door very quietly.

"I'm looking forward to the first meeting between

your sister and my three," said Matthew with relish. "I think it will be a memorable occasion."

Deborah made herself slightly more comfortable and he drew her down on to the sofa, his arm round her.

She looked at him in doubt and passion, her eyes wide and disturbed. "You've known so many other women, Matthew. How can you possibly be sure that whatever you feel for me won't fizzle out as it obviously did with them?"

His hand slid under her breast, warm and comforting, drawing her closer to him. "I'm sure."

"How can you be?"

"I never felt like this before," he said with a glance sideways at her, the sweep of his long black lashes teasing.

"Oh," she murmured, then, breathlessly: "How do you feel?"

He laughed under his breah. "I'm damned if I know how to describe it. I've wanted a woman before with just as much urgency, I suppose, but with you something different happens—a chemical change that makes me race from pure rage to sheer hilarity in a flash. You make me feel alive. With other women the only bond between us was sex. You're different."

She wasn't sure how to take that—as a compliment or an insult. While she was considering it, Matthew went on: "When I met you I was beginning to find life rather boring. Day after day the same old routine—and no end to it, apparently. Identical girls with minds like adding machines seemed to form queues around me. It happens when you've got money. You take them around because there's nothing better to do, but after a while you find yourself forgetting their names, and that's a bad sign."

"It must be," she said drily with a faint bite in her voice, and he laughed again.

"What a nasty little girl you are, at times. When I met you things altered. You made life too lively to give me time to get bored. At first I hardly realised what was happening to me, but when I saw you rolling around on that bed with What's-his-name I got so mad that I realised I was actually jealous of that little swine, and that made me stop short and take a good look at my own feelings." He gave her a wry little grin. "I called in on him in Rome, by the way. I thought I might find you there."

Deborah eyed him. "Poor Rodney! What did you do to him?"

"Bounced him around a little," Matthew admitted with apparent satisfaction. "He soon told me where I could find you."

"That was mean," said Deborah, wishing she had been present. "Poor Rodney," she said again, wondering if Matthew had permanently dented him. Not, of course, that she wished Rodney ill, but she wouldn't be sorry to hear that he had had nightmares since Matthew visited him. Rodney's remark about her being ice from the neck down still stuck in her memory.

Matthew grimaced. "I suppose I must admit to still feeling a bit jealous."

"Of Rodney? You must be insane!" Deborah started to laugh, and Matthew tightened his arm with a dangerous look in his eyes.

"It wasn't funny. If someone had ever told me that I'd be tempted to break a little ferret's neck because I was half out of my mind with jealousy I'd have told him he needed to see a psychiatrist, but the fact remains I felt like chucking your Rodney out of a fifth-storey window until he assured me he wasn't involved with you.''

Deborah was aghast. ''You didn't tell him you were jealous of him? Matt, you must be crazy, you really must! He'll print it. Didn't that occur to you?''

He looked impatiently at her. ''The only thing that occurred to me at the time was that I had to find you and that I had to know you felt the same way I did. I was too busy choking your ferret friend to death to think how it would look in print.''

''You were in a shocking temper,'' she realised with a long, deep sigh, her eyes half amused.

''You shouldn't have run out on me.''

''I had to.''

''Why?'' he demanded, watching her intently. ''I thought I was getting somewhere. Why did you bolt for it?''

''Because you were getting somewhere,'' she admitted, her face flushed. ''I was scared stiff of the way I was beginning to feel and I wasn't going to spend another night alone with you in that villa. I knew the chances were I'd end up in bed with you if I did.''

He looked pleased, his grin broad. ''That's what I thought,'' he said in satisfaction.

''You are the most conceited, irritating...'' she began, and Matthew turned her into his arms and began to kiss her so passionately that she gave up the struggle for articulacy and concentrated on kissing him back.

Harlequin Presents...

The books that let you escape
into the wonderful world of romance!
Trips to exotic places...interesting
plots...meeting memorable people...
the excitement of love....These are
integral parts of Harlequin Presents—
the heartwarming novels read by
women everywhere.

Many early issues are now available.
Choose from this great selection!

Choose from this great selection of exciting Harlequin Presents editions

Relive a great romance...
with Harlequin Presents
Complete and mail this coupon today!

Harlequin Reader Service

In the U.S.A.
1440 South Priest Drive
Tempe, AZ 85281

In Canada
649 Ontario Street
Stratford, Ontario N5A 6W2

Please send me the following Harlequin Presents novels. I am enclosing my check or money order for $1.50 for each novel ordered, plus 75¢ to cover postage and handling.

☐ 99	☐ 103	☐ 109
☐ 100	☐ 106	☐ 110
☐ 101	☐ 107	☐ 111
☐ 102	☐ 108	☐ 112

Number of novels checked @ $1.50 each = $_____

N.Y. and Ariz. residents add appropriate sales tax. $_____

Postage and handling $_____.75

TOTAL $_____

I enclose _____
(Please send check or money order. We cannot be responsible for cash sent through the mail.)

Prices subject to change without notice.

NAME _____
(Please Print)

ADDRESS _____

CITY _____

STATE/PROV. _____

ZIP/POSTAL CODE _____

Offer Expires February 28, 1982.

106563170